COMPELLING EVIDENCE

COMPELLING EVIDENCE

THE KURTHERIAN ENDGAME BOOK TWO

MICHAEL ANDERLE

DISRUPTIVE IMAGINATION®

COMPELLING EVIDENCE TEAM TEAM

Thanks to our Beta Readers

Bree Buras
Dorothy Lloyd
Tom Dickerson
Dorene Johnson
Diane Velasquez
Nat Roberts

Thanks to the JIT Readers

Peter Manis
James Caplan
Daniel Weigert
John Ashmore
Keith Verret
Mary Morris
Kelly O'Donnell
Joshua Ahles

If I've missed anyone, please let me know!

Editor
Lynne Stiegler

To Family, Friends and
Those Who Love
to Read.
May We All Enjoy Grace
to Live the Life We Are
Called.

PROLOGUE

High Tortuga, Hidden Space Fleet Base, The Dome (Formerly the Queen's R&D Lab), Three Months After the Twins' Birth

Bethany Anne closed the door on her guards and locked it behind her. She held up a palm and drew energy from the Etheric to light the hallway. As she walked the hundred and thirty steps to the main chamber, she added energy to the ball until it was as large as her head.

She entered the chamber and released the energy without a thought, muscle memory from the many times she'd made the gesture over the last three months. The ball hit the roof and dissipated into a soft white glow that lit Bethany Anne's way to the seating pad in the center of the cavern.

She dropped her robe and sat down in a huff. "I still think Michael got off too easily."

TOM's voice spoke in her mind. **You knew there was a possibility that the children would mature rapidly.**

1

"Yes, but not so rapidly that they're damned near walking, they *are* talking, and they're potty-trained already! I'd hoped he would get more...*experience*. I'm stuck between feeling bad that we're racing through the early stages and being pissed that Mother Nature is giving him an easy ride after I did my nine months. My lumbar region is *still* complaining."

She shifted on the pad, cozying into the back support, which was made from the same flame-retardant material as the pad. *Lessons had been learned.*

Bethany Anne continued her mini-rant. "When you said it was a likely outcome, I imagined they would grow at a similar rate to Christina—that we'd get at least *some* kind of normal family life."

Are you sure that enjoying Michael's forays into being a modern man is your only motivation?

>>I think it has more to do with the distraction from his dinosaur obsession.<<

Bethany Anne sniffed. "I don't know what you're talking about."

Your brain chemistry tells a different story.

Bethany Anne's tone became momentarily deeper and raspier. "And what is it telling you right *now*?"

I'll get my pillow. TOM spoke in a resigned voice. **Where am I to sleep? The couch?**

"Oh, no." She pointed a finger. "It's the yard for you." When Bethany Anne had awoken to find her Kurtherian tenant some two hundred years ago, one of the first things she'd made sure he understood was what happened to males who pissed off human women. His doghouse might have been metaphorical, but it was *still* well-used.

2

She settled down and rolled her shoulders to loosen the tension. "Be glad I'm not deciding to make it a wet night with a leaky roof. If you must know, I was *hoping* for a little longer with them as babies."

Bethany Anne crossed her legs and let her head drop for a moment, resting her hands on her knees as she put her thoughts in order. "I'm pretty sure that the children are already using the Etheric to communicate mentally with each other and to read us. Alexis in particular. Gabriel is more observant than reactive. So yes, I *am* concerned." She sighed, tapping her lips with a finger. "I wish there was some way to predict what other abilities they are going to develop."

>> **The Pod-cribs are keeping tabs on their development. You are right about Alexis. She has already absorbed most of the curriculum I had prepared for their sleep-learning, and Gabriel is not far behind her.** <<

Bethany Anne smiled. "That's my girl. It's just going so damned *fast*. Every time I turn around one of them has hit a new milestone. You know, I think I'm seeing things a little differently. Maybe staying on-base for a while isn't such a bad choice after all. If they keep growing and learning at this rate, they'll be adults before their third birthday. I don't want to miss any of that."

Mini-adults, maybe. It's more likely that their physical growth will level out once they are fully mobile. Until puberty, that is.

"Do not talk to me about puberty when my babies are only three months old. I am *not* looking forward to when they hit dating age. Can you imagine how Michael will react?"

I fear for any male stupid enough to even breathe the same air as Alexis. And I'm not the only one worried about what will happen when she grows up and introduces someone she's dating to Michael.

"I can imagine it now, 'Hey, Dad, this is (name).'" Bethany Anne made the pantomime of breaking someone's neck. "*Snap.*"

He *is* rather overprotective. You wouldn't let him actually kill some poor boy, though.

She chuckled. "Of course not. But burning his hair off is getting old, and his skills with walking the Etheric have reduced my teaching options drastically."

>>**You did have him going on the whole "intergalactic diaper service" thing for longer than any of us had in the pool.**<<

Bethany Anne snickered. "That was a good one. His face when he found out—" She cut off mid-thought. "Hang on, you were betting?"

>>**Well, yeah. It's kind of what we do for fun around here.**<<

"And you didn't think I'd want a piece of the action?"

>>**It rather defeats the purpose if the person you're betting on knows you're doing it.**<<

"Humph. Some friends *you* two are. See if you like it when I start charging you both rent for living in my body. Maybe I'll remember how much I love the chili here."

TOM whispered to ADAM, **She wouldn't eat it again. She promised! The whole way through the pregnancy it was like I'd been thrown into a volcano.**

>>You do *know* her, right? Distract her, or you're going to be in a world of hurt.<<

TOM focused back on Bethany Anne. **The children will be fine, Bethany Anne. They have you and their father and ADAM and me and...well, I could go on all day. The point is that they have all of us to make sure they are healthy, happy, and well adjusted."**

Bethany Anne's mouth lifted at the corner. "I know, but a mother worries. Besides, the children are a wonderful distraction from Michael's outlandish desire to bring ten tons of dinosaur meat into our home."

She brushed a strand of hair back from her face and straightened her spine. "Speaking of the children. Michael will be getting them ready for their nap soon, which means they will be pulling every trick in the book to *not* take a nap. Shall we get started before they completely destroy their father's sanity?" She closed her eyes and laid her hands flat on her knees. "Ready when you are."

TOM's voice dropped into an almost soothing tone. **Very well. I want you to focus on the Etheric. Immerse yourself in the currents but do not allow yourself to drift, just like we practiced.**

Bethany Anne extended her consciousness and connected with the other dimension's energy. The Etheric swirled in her mind's eye. Layer upon layer of intertwined energy surrounded her; she felt it brush gently against her psyche as if looking to be molded. It welcomed her, wrapping her in its seductive embrace.

As always, there was a moment when the temptation to let go was strong. It would be too easy to allow herself to be carried away by the sense of bliss that connecting on this level stirred in the pit of her stomach.

She anchored herself with the mental image of her children's faces. *I'm in. This is annoying. I'm sick of floating around this place like a* **Gott Verdammt** *ghost every time we practice.* She concentrated hard for a moment, and the tendrils of her consciousness wound themselves into a shadowy Bethany Anne-shaped outline in the mist.

>>**How did you do** *that?*<<

Easy, ADAM. I decided it should happen, and it did. Check this shit out...

She concentrated further and the outline became solid, then features began to form. She snickered at the white noise she was receiving from ADAM and made a final push. She glanced at her hand, which now *looked* like her hand.

TOM chuckled in approval. **Good to know you've been listening. I think you're ready for the next lesson. Examine the strata and tell me what you see.**

She scrutinized the billowing mists. The energy expanded and contracted, forming tight knots that grew denser until they either imploded or exploded. She blinked —or rather, her avatar did—as her brain refused to acknowledge a darker burst of energy which did both. *What the... It's like the world's most fucked-up weather system. There are varying concentrations of energy, all connected to each other. What are they?*

All in good time. Can you sense the pattern of the connections? Where do they lead?

Up ahead. She moved her avatar toward the object of

her attention. *The mist gets darker and more turbulent. Let's get a closer look.*

NO!

The fear in TOM's voice halted Bethany Anne in her tracks. *What's the issue? I'm anchored.*

That is an Etheric storm, Bethany Anne. You don't want to get up close and personal with it, trust me.

She looked at the maelstrom skeptically. *Why not?*

Any number of reasons. Not much is known about the storms—

You don't seem to know much about anything interesting. Maybe I should stick my head in just to see. It's not like I'm really here.

>>You don't want to go in there, BA.<<

What do you know?

ADAM was conspicuously silent.

We will talk about this later. TOM, quit prevaricating and tell me what Kurtherians know about these Etheric storms. What are the dangers here?

There's no danger as long as you do not get entangled in one.

She eyed the boiling mass in the distance, feeling the pull from it. *And what if I do?*

You're not invulnerable. You could be hurt. Not just your psyche, but your body too. Or worse, you could be transported somewhere.

Bethany Anne's eyebrows lifted in surprise. *What? Where?*

Somewhere you are familiar with, maybe? I can't say for certain because the storms are too unpredictable to be harnessed in any practical way.

Meaning your people left them the hell alone?

Got it in one.

ADAM had been quiet during the entire exchange. She turned her attention inward to him and found him regarding the storm.

>>**Curious.**<<

CHAPTER ONE

Unnamed System, Asteroid Field, QBSE _Loralei_, Almost Three Years Later

The sleek search ship drifted in silence. Inside, the EI Loralei didn't sigh. She was in the middle of a report, and she didn't want to be recalled to explain it when High Tortuga received it. "One month expended in this system with no sign of life, Kurtherian or not. However, unlike the last system, this one isn't a total waste of my time. The asteroid belt has rich ore deposits that should be relatively simple to mine. I am including a breakdown of the constituent elements in this report. I will now cloak and create a Gate to move to the next set of coordinates on my list. End report."

She input the required sequence into the Gate drive and shepherded her support probes back inside the ship. "'Go and look for Kurtherians, Loralei,'" she muttered as she sealed them into their docks, downloaded their data and engaged the Gate drive. "'No, we don't know where they are. Just poke around the ass-end of space until you find something.' How did humans even find their way off Earth?"

The plan wasn't actually terrible, and Loralei wasn't *actually* pissed.

However, the ability to spend her time bitching about her directives made the lack of outside stimulation mostly tolerable. Loralei's class of scout ship was designed to cope well with the extended missions, as were the other female EIs who resided in them. Loralei had examined her personality algorithms and was certain that a line here and there had been "borrowed" from Shinigami's original programming.

Consequently, the twelve scout explorer fleet EIs were a bunch of salty bitches (for EIs) who preferred their own company. It helped them deal with the isolation. They didn't need to talk to anyone, and they had almost complete autonomy. The only thing they lacked was the ability to develop emotion. While Loralei and her sisters could never ascend to AI status, they were the next best thing. Loralei might not feel, but she *could* react appropriately to whatever situation she found herself in.

Nobody wanted another AI to suffer the way Ricky Bobby had.

The *Loralei* emerged in a very different system to the one it had left. Loralei plotted a wide arc around the outward boundary of the system and began a new report. "First impressions are that I might actually have a little fun here. We have a red dwarf star with three surrounding bodies, and there are signs of life on the outermost planet.

Initiating scans now and moving in to examine the other two planets."

She released the majority of her probes and sent them off in all directions to gather information about the rest of the system while she went to check out the planets. Loralei chose to conceal her ship's signature—or rather, the lack of one—from the life forms on the third planet until she knew more about them. The long-range sensors enabled Loralei to keep a safe distance.

Loralei scanned the planet closest to the star. "Deader than a dead thing that is dead. There's no sign life ever existed here. No atmosphere, not even any bacteria to make soil. I calculate that's because the planet has never been within the habitable zone of the star, or if it was, then it was billions of years ago."

The EI moved on to the second planet, noting a debris field between it and the outermost planet. "I am detecting the remains of a reasonably advanced civilization on this planet. There are no life signs, however, and the atmosphere is no longer conducive to supporting life. Moving on."

The *Loralei* crossed the debris field, weaving around crystallized chunks of space rock. Her sensors pinged. "Oh. Wasn't expecting that. My sensors are picking up the signature of worked metal. Moving in to investigate. Encrypting transmission now." Loralei curbed the ship's speed to approach cautiously and prepared her message torp to send back just in case.

She received a broken burst from one of her probes, and then another. Then they all went dark at once. Loralei calculated the possible reasons. There was something fishy going on here. She didn't take the possibility of destruction into consideration. High Tortuga wouldn't receive her transmission in time to save her if the shit hit the fan since the *Loralei* didn't have Etheric connectivity. However, they *would* know where to retrieve her ship from when they got her message.

The ship's warning system told Loralei there was incoming. "Whoever is hearing this, it looks like I'm in a jam. It's a good thing I can't panic because all my sensors have just lit up." Loralei scanned for an escape route. She spotted a gap in the debris, spun her ship on its axis, and dropped into the layer of dust below. "Readying defenses and priming Gate drive."

Scanners picked up a burst of energy just as a ship came hurtling out of a gap in the cloud. It was coming straight toward her, led by a spread of missiles. Loralei picked up a brief blip behind the strange ship on her sensors. It sped away too fast to track, but Loralei got a lock on it long enough to ascertain that it was headed away from them. "*Dammit*, they got a communication out."

Loralei sent a wave of kinetics out to destroy the missiles coming toward her, but even her pucks couldn't match the speed of the whatever-it-was heading in the opposite direction. There was no issue with the missiles coming toward her. The pucks met the missiles in a shower of bright flashes that lit the dust around the two ships.

The *Loralei* shook as one made it through and scored a hit on her flank. "I've taken a hit. Calculating damage. Shit. The Gate drive is offline." Loralei scanned the ship as it passed her position and she was blocked. "Double dammit.

They have an EI. Preparing to repair Gate drive and get the hell out of here."

The enemy ship flipped and came directly at the *Loralei*.

"No way. I think the crazy bastard is going to ram me. Gate drive has failed. My calculations are telling me I'm not going to make it out of this." This time Loralei allowed herself to sigh. "A Queen Bitch's EI got to do what a Queen Bitch's EI got to do. If I'm not making it out of here? Then neither are *they*."

Loralei swung her vessel around and set a course for the nose of the enemy ship. She embedded an encrypted copy of her report in a message torp, a tiny torpedo programmed to return to a predesignated destination where it would feed the data back to High Tortuga via the Etheric. "I hope you all appreciate what I'm doing here. I sure as hell wish I had a few motherpuckers right now. When you come out here and drag my crumpled ass back, you make sure to load me up with some before I get sent back out again."

The *Loralei* met the enemy ship nose-on.

A short time later a small, unmanned torp cruised over the remains of the two ships. The onboard EI scanned the wreckage thoroughly, paying extra attention to what remained of the *Loralei*. The alien torp completed its circuit, turned, and shot out of the opposite end of the system in a flash of blue light.

Seventh Planet, Gahl System, Prime Spaceport Meeting Room 43a

General Lance Reynolds tapped his fingers on the table

and stared impassively at the bickering Noel-ni before him.

Beneath the calm exterior he was more than a little pissed at the delay in getting the hell off this planet, but just the same, he'd rearranged his departure to accept the "urgent" request for an audience he'd received from the Noel-ni delegation that morning.

Reia, the leader of the delegation, arrived on time with her entourage and had been about to tell him the reason for their visit when another group of Noel-ni entered and started an argument with the delegates.

Lance had broken up the dispute before it came to blows, and now he had two groups of bristling Noel-ni facing off across his conference table.

He sighed inwardly, wishing he was allowed to smoke in here. Half the reason he'd chewed that cigar all those years was so he could bite back his temper when *stupid shit* like this occurred.

He tapped the table. "Look, I'm a busy man. You need to give me some clue as to why you're here taking up my time, or I'm going to have to ask you all to leave."

The leader of the delegation dragged her glare from the Noel-ni opposite and turned her head to look at Lance. Her expression was only a little less hostile than it had been when she was facing her rival. "We are here because we have a problem."

"Nothing we need human help with!" the rival exclaimed. "Keep them out of it, Reia!"

Reia rounded on the unfortunate male. She leaned over the table and slashed his face with a swipe of her claws. He dodged, but not quickly enough. "If we didn't need help I would not be here asking for it, you fool. Besides, we are asking for the *Federation's* assistance. You will be silent, Drazen, or you will be removed from your position permanently." He narrowed his eyes and bared his teeth, but did as he was told.

Reia turned back to Lance. "We recently lost contact with two freighters carrying goods vital to a trade agreement we have with the Q'Palmeretta. Their escort also dropped out of communication. We sent ships to investigate, but they vanished also."

"What does that have to do with the Federation?" Lance frowned and took a sip of his expertly blended single malt. He might not be able to smoke, but God bless Bobcat for the Scotch.

"Unless we deliver the trade goods, the treaty will be broken, and we will be at war with the Q'Palmeretta." Reia's lip curled slightly. She put an organically secured memory chip on the table and pushed it over to Lance. "This is all the data we have. All we know is that it happened just outside the boundary of Federation space. The Noel-ni are members of the Federation, General. If we go to war, the Federation goes to war. You're the head of the Federation, so do something about it before we end up in that position."

Lance steepled his hands on the table in front of him. "You getting your asses in a sling doesn't mean the Federation has to jump in, and you know it." He leaned forward to put a finger on the chip. "However, leave it with me. I'll get to the bottom of it."

He really *didn't* want a war breaking out with the

Q'Palmeretta. He had two agents in their area right now trying to reduce other tensions the Leath had kicked up.

If it wouldn't give Bethany Anne ideas, he would go to the Leath and put his boot up their asses. They needed to keep their "business" groups on a shorter leash.

Reia stood and nodded, then swept from the meeting room, followed by her entourage. The rival with the bloody muzzle was the last to leave. He slunk after the others with an almost defeated slump to his shoulders, turning back as he exited to steal a baleful glance at Lance.

Lance returned to the ship and began his investigation from there. Home was only a few hours away. Besides, he wanted to dig into that Drazen character a little. There was something off about him; something more than the standard Noel-ni aversion to anyone who wasn't a Noel-ni.

When he reached his office on his ship, he sat at his desk and slid the top drawer open. He removed a slim wooden box, then placed it on his desk and turned his chair around to retrieve the decanter and a cut-glass tumbler from the sideboard behind him.

He turned on his terminal, poured a measure into his glass, and removed a cigar from the wooden box. He cut the end and inhaled the rich aroma of the tobacco, savoring the silence and the rare opportunity to enjoy a cigar without Patricia looking at him like he'd just done something horrible on the living room carpet while her book club was there.

He completely agreed that he shouldn't smoke around baby Kevin, so it was a luxury he hadn't had for a while.

Especially since he'd been stuck on the no-fun political world for the last couple of weeks. At least that was over now, and he had something more suited to his preferences to deal with. He hated the endless rounds of meetings, memos, and whiny civil servants up his ass that his role as head of the Federation had landed him in.

How life had changed from the simple days back on the Colorado base, when he only had to worry about the soldiers under his command and the day-to-day demands of running the base.

Of course, he wouldn't exchange what he had now for anything, trade conferences on puritan worlds notwithstanding.

Lance considered the potential clusterfuck while he scrolled through the data Reia had given him.

This was the first real challenge to the nascent Federation where the ex-Empress wasn't waiting in the wings to scare the miscreant children into behaving. He knew a call to Bethany Anne could resolve the issue with no blowback on the Federation, but he was the one in charge now.

His daughter needed time to raise her family, and do whatever else she was doing over on the planet that couldn't make up its mind about its damn name.

It was also the first opportunity for Lance to begin cementing the shaky foundation they were resting their hopes for a brighter future on into place. A chance to build trust between the edgy factions who had spent generations upon generations doing their best to screw each other over.

No, there would be no calling Bethany Anne. There was a minute chance that she'd listen to Michael, so he decided that he would risk her finding out; he'd call him and ask for his help keeping her out of it.

The Federation needed to put on their big-boy pants before Bethany Anne heard what was going on and decided she should motivate them with a tickle of the toes she used to kick their asses with.

It was probably best that didn't happen. He got back to work on the information from the Noel-ni delegate.

CHAPTER TWO

High Tortuga, Space Fleet Base, Queen's Suite

Bethany Anne snuggled into Michael's shoulder with a satisfied smile on her face. "The children will be awake soon." She got out of bed and dressed quickly, flinging one arm into her robe, then the other.

Not quickly enough.

Michael glided up behind her, almost too quietly for her to hear. He wrapped his arms around her waist and rested his chin on her shoulder. "But they are not awake yet..."

Bethany Anne turned in his arms and kissed him soundly. "You must be getting deaf in your old age, my love." She danced out of his reach and tied her robe.

As if on cue, Alexis and Gabriel burst into their room. Alexis dashed to the bed and began bouncing up and down like a tiny whirlwind. Gabriel ran straight to Michael and crushed his leg in a brief hug before attaching himself firmly to Bethany Anne's side.

Their growth had slowed significantly shortly after they were able to walk around by themselves, just as TOM had predicted. They looked more like six-year-olds, and were precocious learners.

Bethany Anne looked at Michael. *How did they get this big already?*

We gifted them with the best genes in existence, my dear.

I can hear you, Alexis interrupted, her little eyes staring at her parents as she stopped jumping on their bed.

Michael tilted his head a little and affected a stern look. "Alexis, remember how we talked about not listening in on Mommy's and Daddy's private conversations?"

"It's our birthday, Daddy," Alexis told him, straight-faced. "You can't be mad on our birthday!" She tilted her head and gave him her mother's eyes.

Michael was helpless. He knelt and held his arms out to her. "It is indeed, my little princess. Shall we get ready for breakfast?"

"You're a sucker for a pair of wide eyes," Bethany Anne called after them as they left the room.

"How do you think *you* snared me?" he called back over his shoulder as Alexis threw herself into the air.

Bethany Anne smiled until she heard the rest of his remark inside her mind.

Did you think it was your chipper attitude on that mountain all those years ago?

Bethany Anne's smile dropped. *Just get your ass to the kitchen.*

This time it was Gabriel who interjected, *Mommy, I can hear you!* He laughed and ran ahead of her up the short corridor. "Mommy said 'ass,' Mommy said 'ass!'"

Bethany Anne rolled her eyes. *She really needed to get a handle on her potty mouth.* "I think it's time to get a swear jar," she murmured.

Soft lighting came on overhead automatically when they entered the kitchen. Alexis and Gabriel turned as one to their parents.

"Yes, go play," Bethany Anne told them. "We'll call when breakfast is ready." She went to the fridge and began stacking ingredients on the counter.

The twins ran through the kitchen, across the family area, and through the left door to the playroom.

Michael snagged an apron from the hook by the stove. "You remembered the berries? And the syrup?"

"As if I'd forget! The blueberries were easy. I just put in a call to Agritopia. The maple syrup, however, was *not* easy to source. You can thank Stephen. He was very tight-lipped about where he got it, though." She passed him a griddle from the low cupboard and headed for the dressing room to pick their outfits for the day.

She paused in the doorway and looked back at him. "I love how domestic you've become."

Michael patted the pancake in the pan a little too hard. "I am not *domestic*," he muttered under his breath as he worked the spatula to save the pancake. *"I am a force of nature which cannot be contained."*

Bethany Anne smirked. "Yes, dear." She crossed the divided room, grabbing a few items for herself and Michael as she passed their everyday wardrobe and went into the twins' shared closet space at the back.

This was her favorite part of family life. Almost every morning they went through this ritual of waking up and eating breakfast together, a little pocket of the day that was just for the four of them.

She ran her hand over the rack holding all of Alexis' clothing—from her much loved jeans and completely unworn dresses and pretty tops, all the way to the end of the rail where her daughter's favorite outfits hung. She smiled, seeing a teaching opportunity.

Parenting a child with abilities like her own came with the expected challenges. Parenting twins came with a set all its own. The children needed to be occupied from morning until night. Not necessarily supervised, but definitely occupied.

ADAM had come up with a rigorous learning schedule that took into account both the children's age, the differences in their learning methods, and their constant need to absorb new information.

Alexis was a logical learner, as opposed to Gabriel's kinesthetic style. She grasped each new experience as though it were her last breath, dismantled it, and came to her own conclusions about what she'd learned, sometimes with unintended consequences. Last week she'd accidentally switched on the ability to communicate telepathically with others besides her brother and had begun broadcasting her thoughts to anyone who could hear. Bethany Anne had been working with her since then to strengthen the ability and bring it under control.

Alexis?

Yes, Mommy?

Show me the atmosuit you want to wear today and tell me which one you don't.

Ummm... There was a pause, in which Bethany Anne

caught a brief impression of purple sparkles from Alexis before it merged into a muddy brown. *Orange ruffles, please, Mommy.*

She grabbed the purple atmosuit, impressed by her daughter's control. *That was much better than last time, sweetie! Uncle Barnabas will be super-impressed when I tell him how quickly you're working this stuff out.*

Alexis had a squeal in her inner voice. *Really?*

Yes. I have your purple sparkles. Well done, sweetheart. She grabbed the atmosuit, as well as one for Gabriel, who wore blue every day regardless. She made her way back to the kitchen, which was filled with the delicious aroma of blueberry pancakes.

She waited until Michael wasn't near the flame and repaid his sneak attack from earlier with one of her own. She wrapped her arms around his waist and squeezed. "Mmmm," she mumbled into his ear, reaching around him to swipe a blueberry from the bowl beside him. "That smell makes me want to go back in time and marry you all over again."

Michael flipped the pancakes one at a time. "If you work out how to do that, let me know. I fudged the last batch."

There was a pause behind him as Bethany Anne turned. *"Fudged?"*

Michael nodded, flipping the pancake. "Did you hear the words from our infant son's mouth? Fudged. I don't think a swear jar is a bad idea, but we'll have to make it interesting..."

Bethany Anne grinned and let go. "What have you got in mind?"

Michael pressed down on the pancakes, gently this time. "I'm not sure yet. It will wait, I have something else to tell you. Don't overreact—"

"Said by every man about to deliver news sure to make the recipient sh...have kittens." She popped the blueberry into her mouth and sat on a stool at the breakfast bar across from him. "So what's this news I'm supposed to not overreact to?"

Michael slid the pancakes onto a platter and carried it to the table. "Your dad and Patricia can't make it for the party."

Bethany Anne had gotten up to bring the rest of the breakfast items over, and her eyes narrowed. "No? Why not?"

"He's having some kind of issue. He's not sure what the root cause is yet, so he doesn't believe it would be prudent to leave the Federation."

"I wonder if it's the Leath? Who am I kidding? Of course, it is."

Michael raised an eyebrow. This was exactly what Lance had wanted to avoid, and why he'd called Michael instead of her. "It could be outside influences. We don't know that it's the Leath. Don't be so quick to jump to conclusions."

She stopped and stared at him. "It's hard *not* to. I might have to go and investigate if he can't resolve it through legal channels. It would be just like those...those... *Verdammt*, how hard can it be to curse without cursing?"

Michael chuckled dryly. "I'm sure your vocabulary will improve as you find new ways to further besmirch our language."

She pursed her lips. "I didn't realize I was so off my game. The Leath, those sneaky, two-faced ingrates. It would be just like them to stir up trouble. Please remind me again why I didn't just wipe them out?"

"Because your days as a sociopathic goddess of death are over, my love." He placed a steaming pancake on her plate. "Want to let our children know breakfast is ready?"

"No need, Daddy," Alexis chirped from the doorway.

Gabriel followed her in. "We smelled the pancakes."

High Tortuga, Space Fleet Base, Base Rec Room Omega 3

"Shhh, you'll wake him up."

Tabitha snickered and stepped back, admiring her work. "I doubt it. Cheryl Lynn was in a *fantastic* mood this morning. Glowing, I'd say. Scotty-boy is sleeping the sleep of the well and truly—"

Scott jerked awake, and all the paper cups, disposable cutlery, various items of food and clothing that Tabitha, John, Peter, and Eric had spent the last twenty minutes balancing on his sleeping body fell to the floor.

He caught the donut Tabitha had just placed on his head as it fell and demolished half of it in one bite. "Assholes."

ADAM cut in from the speaker beside them, "They're on their way. Positions, everyone!"

Everyone was in place ten seconds before Bethany Anne and Michael came in with the children.

"Surprise!" they all yelled.

Alexis looked around the group with a happy smile. "Well, actually..."

Tabitha dropped to one knee, and two gift-wrapped parcels appeared in her hands. "Come and see what your fun Aunt Tabbie got for you."

Alexis and Gabriel didn't need to be asked twice.

Alexis squealed when she opened the shoe box. "Thank you!" She pulled out the glittery combat boots and held them up to her face. "How did you know?"

Tabitha grinned and tapped the side of her nose with a finger. "Your Aunt Tabbie *always* knows."

You saw them when she was broadcasting last week, Peter pointed out.

Tabitha narrowed her eyes at him over the top of Alexis' head. *Don't you dare ruin my image as the fun aunt, Peter! My revenge will not be sweet—at least not for you!*

Peter raised his hands and took half a step back with a smirk on his face.

Gabriel opened his next. His eyes lit up when he opened the slim box and saw the contents. "Is this an upgrade for my app suite?"

Tabitha nodded. "Yes. Achronyx helped me. It's a whole new toolset. It's compatible across all your devices."

Gabriel gazed up at her in total adoration. "It works with the IRT-Pod?" Tabitha nodded. His mouth worked as he tried to find words. He settled for throwing his arms around her legs. "You're the *best*! Thank you, Aunt Tabbie!"

Akio came forward with a pair of longish boxes.

Bethany Anne had a good idea of what was in the boxes, and she put up a hand. "Please tell me you're not gifting my children with weapons already, Akio."

Akio inclined his head slightly. "It is my honor to present them with their first blades. I will also teach them to use them." *Also,* he sent mentally, *these are practice blades. No edge. They have to earn that.*

Bethany Anne and Michael looked at each other and exchanged a minute nod.

Akio knelt and held out a box to each child. "We will begin your education tomorrow."

Alexis perked up at the mention of study. Gabriel was transfixed by the child-sized sword in the box.

"We will take care of those for you," Michael told them firmly.

"We can't spar with them now?" Gabriel looked up at his dad, disappointed.

Bethany Anne smiled at her son. "You won't want to when you see who's just getting here."

Gabriel and Alexis gazed at her. "Who?" they asked in unison.

Bethany Anne smiled. "You have two minutes to try to get it from my mind before they get here."

"So it's a 'they?'" Alexis asked. "Hmm…"

Bethany Anne felt both of them try to probe her mind to find the answer. Gabriel screwed his little face up in concentration, and her heart melted.

"Ashur!" Alexis shouted. "Ashur is coming!"

Bethany Anne looked at her children in shock. "Did you two just *play* me?"

Gabriel gave her a cheeky smile. "It's like you always say, Mommy—the only fair fight is the fight you *lose.*"

John let out a rumbling chuckle. "Pretty sure someone said that before you, BA."

Bethany Anne made a face as she put a hand to her forehead, wincing. "Oh my God, I've become my dad."

The children ran off to meet Ashur, and Bethany Anne left Michael to catch up with Akio while she grabbed a Coke from the wet bar.

She came back a moment later to hear him bitching to his oldest friend about his latest nemesis. "Are you *still* going on about that damn T-rex?"

Michael huffed. "I would have caught one already if *someone* hadn't placed so many restrictions on my hunt."

Bethany Anne smiled thinly. "Can't have you destroying half the planet on some insane whim, so no explosives. Can't be seen to interfere in the planet's ecosystem, so only an older male with no more value to the breeding population." She had found that last part inspired. ADAM had predicted that the likelihood of Michael bringing home the dino-bacon had gone way down with *that* little rule.

He appeared to know it, too. "You know that the aging males are the most aggressive, my love."

"Then you had better continue to be extremely careful not to get killed, *my love*." She turned and left him to his complaints, heading after the children.

From the sound of it, Ashur hadn't come alone. She followed the tinkle of her children's laughter, which was mingled with a series of high-pitched yips. The yips were being emitted by two smoke-gray puppies.

Bethany Anne winked at Bellatrix. "I see you got your way."

Ashur chuffed, and the puppies jumped to attention. "Zeus, Athena, come and meet my human. Bethany Anne, meet the puppies."

Bethany Anne bent to offer them her hands to snuffle.

Hello, large human, Athena greeted her.

Oh, you can speak mind-to-mind.

We both can, Zeus informed her.

"Interesting." She arched an eyebrow at Ashur, who shook his head. She held out her hands to the children. "We will see. Ready for your gifts?"

"Can we play with the puppies for a little while first?" Gabriel asked.

"Pleeease?" Alexis chimed in, her little hands clasped together.

The puppies gave Ashur their cutest looks. "I will stay with them," Ashur laid down.

Bethany Anne smiled at the four hopeful faces. "Okay, but don't go far."

"We won't, Mommy," the twins promised.

"And stay where I can hear you!" Bethany Anne added.

They nodded rapidly, their eyes already on the large space beyond the doors where they could run free. "We will!"

Conversation in the main room had turned to the question that had been stumping them for the last three years. Michael looked up as Bethany Anne entered the room.

She smiled at him and grabbed a fresh Coke on her way to join everybody at the table. "So has anyone found a place for our rebels to thrive? Or are we still turning it over?"

Judging by the sighs, it was the latter. "It can't be this hard to find a suitable planet! We've been searching for a while now. Everything else has run mostly smoothly. We have the control we need over the shipping industry, and the libraries are working even better than we could have imagined... But the rebels; the outcasts. The ones I won't leave behind. They aren't happy."

"It's not from lack of trying," Peter assured her. "We pull them from the testing process and treat any existing medical or mental health issues that account for their inability to work within the construct of society. We integrate many of them back into society."

Tabitha nodded. "Those people would have fallen through the cracks in any of the old systems," she agreed. "But there are still some who can't easily live under the rules of society, and we promised ourselves we would work like hell to figure out a place for everyone."

Bethany Anne set her bottle on a table and twisted it slightly as she considered the thorny problem for the millionth time. "We need to look at this from a different angle. It's pretty much the only thing holding us back from the next phase of hiding this planet."

Michael cut in, "We've looked at it from *all* the angles, and at least when we *do* find a planet, we're pretty much ready to go." He gazed around for a moment in thought. "I think we need a break from this planet."

Bethany Anne considered briefly. "That works. I would like to see my baby brother."

"I was thinking more along the lines of date night," Michael replied. "There *has* to be somewhere to go out in space, but close to here, yes?"

"Who would take care of the children?" A sea of hands rose. Bethany Anne's mouth twitched. "Okay, point taken. Leave it to me."

Ashur came trotting into the room. He looked all around, his head tilted in confusion. "Where are the children?" he chuffed. "They were right in front of me, I swear."

Bethany Anne was in the hallway before Ashur's translator had finished speaking. "Kids? *Alexis? Gabriel?*"

Michael was at her side in a heartbeat. "Children, come out now. You're worrying your mother!" He looked around again and turned to Bethany Anne. "I will check at home. They may have taken the puppies to the playroom." The next moment, he was gone.

Bethany Anne searched for her children's mental signatures, but couldn't locate either of them. Her heart rose into her mouth. "Where are my babies? ADAM!"

Silence.

"*ADAM!* Get your ass out here! Where are you, dammit?"

"Maybe the base EI could help," John offered. CEREBRO, locate Alexis and Gabriel."

The EI came back a six agonizing seconds later. "They are not in the base."

"What do you mean, they're not in the base?" Bethany Anne demanded. Her eyes blazed red, and the air around her began to crackle dangerously. *"Where the fuck are my children?"*

Ashur came over and put his head against her thigh. She reached down automatically to bury her hand in his fur. As she did so, her connection to the Etheric strengthened. She looked down at Ashur, then at John. "You don't think..."

John's brow furrowed. "What?"

His question had been posed to empty air.

A moment later, she was back with a child in each arm and two very confused puppies. Ashur immediately hustled both puppies in the direction of their mother.

Michael appeared. "What happened? Where were they?"

"I found them wandering the Etheric," she told him. "I have no idea how it happened."

"It was Zeus, daddy."

His eyes widened, and he opened his arms to gather the three of them up. "Alexis." His charcoal eyes turned to his son. "Gabriel. Moving to the other dimension without us is *not* allowed. This *isn't* open for discussion."

"We didn't do it on purpose!" Gabriel protested.

Alexis was about to join him when a big yawn came out of her mouth.

Bethany Anne nuzzled her cheek. "Someone is ready for her nap."

Alexis didn't argue, for once.

That's unusual.

She went into the Etheric. It was a big adventure, even if it was only for a few minutes.

She shifted the weight of the sleepy children on her hips. *Michael?*

Yes?

How are we going to put a child lock on the Etheric?

CHAPTER THREE

High Tortuga, Space Fleet Base, Prime Building, Michael's Office

Michael muted the screen and crossed his office. He skirted William's feet, which were sticking out from underneath the VR stage he'd had installed shortly after Bethany Anne had imposed her little constraints upon his hunt. "Well?"

William scooted out from the silent machinery and shook his head sadly. "My official diagnosis is that you fucked it up." He got up and dusted himself off. "I can get it fixed, but if you're gonna keep Mysting into the works, it's gonna keep happening."

A faint line appeared on Michael's brow. "Doesn't matter. I'm done with training."

William raised an eyebrow, then went over to the fridge and stuck his head in. "Don't you have any beer down here?" He pulled his head out of the fridge and looked back at Michael, who shook his head and pointed at the bar cabinet by the seating area. "You're ready?"

Michael shrugged. "I was ready three years ago. It just took this long to find a worthy opponent that also fit the criteria set by my beloved." He glanced at the screen, which was set to track his chosen quarry around the clock. He was an elusive beast, for one so large and aggressive. "However, I still do not possess a place to *cook* my kill, a situation for which I hope you have a remedy, William. How is my pit coming along?"

William grinned. "It's coming just fine. I addressed and solved the issue we were having with maintaining even temperature over such a large area. The replacement components have been built, and you know that the rest of it has been ready to go for a while. I just need you to tell me where to install the damn thing so I can get my workshop back."

Michael frowned. "I thought we had already decided that? Down by the kitchens, where the smell can be vented."

William shook his head, his eyes wide. "Yeah, *no*. BA visited my workshop the other day. She had different instructions, and I'm way more scared of her than I am you, so..." He lifted a shoulder. "Just sayin'."

Michael's mouth twitched. "And what did my beloved demand? Uh, *decree*?"

"She said, and I quote, 'If you put that fucking grill *anywhere* I can smell the meat cooking, the first thing that's getting cooked on it are your balls.'" William thought for a moment, looking at the ceiling. "I'm not sure if she meant my balls or yours, but I'm not willing to take the risk that she meant mine. You should pick another place since she probably meant us both."

Michael winced. "I think finding a location away from the base may be a wise move. Somewhere Bethany Anne cannot possibly gripe about."

William considered the options. "So, on another continent, then?"

"Of course not," Michael replied. A slight smile touched his lips. "Which means yes."

William chuckled and helped himself to a drink. He held up an empty glass to Michael, who shook his head.

William walked over to the couch and sat back. "So how are you going to kill this thing? I watched the playback on your VR, and it kinda looked like you were losing badly." He waited for the rebuke, which didn't come. He grinned at Michael. "I gotta say, I'm not the only one enjoying this new more chilled you."

Michael raised an eyebrow and pressed his lips together.

William held up a hand. "Okay, I'm not pushing it. But seriously, this fucker is fifty feet tall and nasty as hell. How do you expect to take him down?"

Michael waved him off, then looked at his hand as though it belonged to someone else. His wife, maybe? "Oh, that's not an issue. I've thought of hundreds of ways to do it."

"Name three."

"I could use the Etheric in any number of ways to take him down." His face hardened as he spoke. "I've just been playing these last few months; refining my approach."

"Even with all of BA's rules?"

Another stony look.

William cracked up at that. "Ohhh, that's *priceless*. You never intended to abide by them, did you?" He wiped away a tear. "You'll never get away with ignoring her."

Michael made a slight dismissive sound. "I just nodded along. She didn't set any constraints I wouldn't have held myself to anyway. By her lights, it would be completely acceptable to simply Myst through the beast and leave a grenade in his heart. There's no honor in that. Plus, it would spoil the meat."

William blinked a couple of times before his eyebrows slanted together. "Why do you bring honor into just about everything?"

Michael put his hands behind his back. "To fight on equal terms is honorable, no matter the opponent. It will be a match of my wits against the raw aggression of nature. It has been too long since I experienced that."

"You have a fair amount of raw aggression yourself," William commented. "It's not going to save you if the damn thing smooshes you under his foot."

The corner of Michael's mouth lifted ever so slightly. "Then I will just have to be faster than the dinosaur." He held up a hand coated in Etheric energy and flashed a wicked grin. "Besides, I don't plan on him being able to stand long enough to 'smoosh' me."

"So you're going old-school?" William snickered and raised his glass when Michael nodded. "You know, you're pretty badass for a white dude."

The thousand-years-plus vampire looked at the behemoth on the screen, and his lip curled to reveal one gleaming fang. "I'm *white?*"

High Tortuga, Space Fleet Base, Prime Building, One Week Later

Bethany Anne took one more look at the angelic faces of her children. They slept soundly in their Pod-cribs, which were less like cribs and more like mini-bunks in their fourth iteration, since Eve kept coming up with improvements to their functionality.

She switched the nightlight on and left the nursery.

Her next stop was her closet. Not the one she shared with the family, the one that belonged exclusively to her. The space had been built by Jean, with all of Bethany Anne's preferences in mind. Even Michael was not permitted to enter her haven, which had gone down with him as expected until she'd reminded him that a little mystery in a relationship was a good thing.

"You have shoes in there, don't you?" had been his first question.

She hadn't deigned to answer.

A wave of her hand opened the door, and she stepped into the anteroom with the same warm feeling she always had when she entered the combination sitting room and shrine to her Louboutin collection.

The shoe collection was all that remained of her not-so-secret hoard. In two hundred years of continually kicking someone's ass, she'd gone through a *lot* of shoes.

When she'd gotten down to the last five hundred pairs or so, she'd had them all packed and stored to keep them in perfect condition.

They were the last Louboutins in existence, after all.

Jean had barely raised an eyebrow at her request, which Bethany Anne had appreciated. However, there was no way she was letting Michael in here. One look at the lighted display cases recessed into the walls, and she would never hear the end of it—which would be a very long time indeed. Especially since she'd spent the last three years riding his ass about his dinosaur obsession.

You okay? TOM asked as her hand touched a few pairs.

Sure. Memories, that's all. She swept down the corridor to her dressing rooms, taking the right-hand door when she reached it.

The war room?

She took her swords down from the rack to her left as she entered and laid them on the table that was ten feet away in the center of the room. *Yup.*

I could swear you told Michael this was date night. I thought you were planning a pleasant evening out?

I am. She selected a few more blades and laid them alongside the swords, then the box with her Jean Dukes Specials. *I'm planning a pleasant evening of ass-kicking. It's been too long since we just cut loose, and ADAM found us the perfect place to do it.*

Say no more.

She stacked her armor plates, pulled off her pants, and yanked her top over her head. Her chest plate went on easily, as did the ones for her torso, arms, and legs. *Damn back plate. Why did I never get something made that could hold this fucking bit still while I get it on?* She got it into place on the third attempt. *Is that on?* She arched her upper back, and the plate stayed where she'd placed it. *Thank fuck for that.*

What happened to cutting out the cursing? TOM's voice held an edge of amusement.

I'm not cursing where my children can hear me. I never said a thing about keeping it clean in the privacy of my own mind.

TOM snickered and was gone. She grabbed her leathers from the hangers and dressed quickly, but hesitated when it came to choosing her footwear. Her combat boots were the obvious choice, given where they were going.

However, this was date night. Ass-kicking capabilities aside, she wanted something a little more...dressy. She reached for the over-the-knee boots she'd had made a year previously during a phase of cabin fever that had seen both her wardrobe and her personal armory expand.

The boots had been one of her more practical commissions.

The leather came from a creature native to High Tortuga. Its hide was all but impenetrable, but also as supple as suede—which made them perfect for looking the part while she was busy being a badass.

Procuring the hide to make the boots had distracted Michael from his barbecue fantasies for a good month and a half, and their ability to distract her husband hadn't ended there.

She smirked and checked that the retractable blade in the heel was safe before she pulled them on. Next, she slid on her double back harness and fastened her holsters to her belt, then filled them with the weapons she'd laid out, saving her swords for last.

She slid them into the back harness, flicked her hair

back, and left the closet in search of Michael, pausing only to grab a sword for him.

She found him at the breakfast bar in the kitchen, engrossed in watching something on a tablet. He was dressed in evening wear, and his shoes would definitely not withstand the night she had planned. A tinny roar from the speaker told her everything she needed to know.

Damn dinosaur.

She narrowed her eyes and tossed the extra sword she'd brought in his direction. "Catch!"

Michael looked up from his screen and plucked the sword out of the air. He placed it on the breakfast bar and looked down at the soft shirt and pressed trousers he was wearing with a slightly rueful expression. "Oh, it's *that* kind of date night."

He came over and wrapped his arms around her. "What happened to dinner?"

"We wouldn't want to break tradition *now*, would we?" She leaned into her husband and inhaled his familiar scent. "Besides, you're going to love what I have planned. One word." She pressed her mouth to his ear and whispered, "*Pirates.*"

She felt his mouth quirk against her jaw.

"You've never disappointed me yet, my love. Give me a few minutes to change." He kissed her cheek and headed out of the kitchen.

Bethany Anne took a moment to appreciate the view as Michael left. It was a shame about those pants. They fit him so nicely.

She considered following him, but her fight gear had been enough of a PITA to get into the first time. She would just have to get him to help her out of it when they were done with the date.

ADAM, is the ship ready?

>>The *ArchAngel II* is ready to go. She's just waiting for you to arrive.<<

Michael returned a couple of minutes later, his elegant evening wear replaced by something a bit tougher and certainly easier to clean the blood off of.

Bethany Anne raised an eyebrow. "No hat?"

Michael smirked and reached into the Etheric. His hand returned holding his black hat and duster.

Bethany Anne pursed her lips. "I approve." She waved a finger towards the front. "Do you mind getting the door? Our sitter is here."

The Bethany Anne's words had barely left her mouth when Michael opened the door. His eyebrows narrowed as he looked John up and down. "Are you expecting an attack while we are away?" Michael asked.

John followed Michael's gaze to his weapons. "What? No." He waved into the suite. "I was told we should be ready for a fight?"

Jean pushed past Michael into the suite and made her way to the kitchen. "Damned thing's heavy!" She put a bulky crate on the breakfast bar beside Bethany Anne, who eyed the crate, then the R&D specialist. "All ready to go! Or at least you will be if the men quit jacking their jaws and you three get out of here."

Jean lifted the lid of the crate a little and took out a small box, handing it to Bethany Anne. "Just like we discussed." She looked around, a question written on her face.

"Where are my niece and nephew?" she asked.

Bethany Anne pointed at the twins' bedroom door. "Missed your chance. They'll be asleep for the next few hours. If it's a bust, we'll be back before they wake up, but they're expecting you to be here if we're not."

Jean grinned. "You just take your sweet time." She patted the crate. "I've been looking forward to some quality aunt time with the children. Tabitha gets all the damn glory."

Bethany Anne frowned and looked down. "What's in the crate, Jean?"

Grinning, Jean tapped the side of her nose with a finger. "'Secret aunt stuff.'" She shook her finger at Bethany Anne. "Don't think I've forgotten how you pulled that crap with Lillian. And Nickie too, come to think about it."

Bethany Anne rolled her eyes and sighed. "I suppose I earned this."

"Oh, you *know* you earned it. Karma's a bitch, BA." She snickered and shooed Bethany Anne toward the door.

"Just remember, so am I. And this bitch has been feeling a little insecure since her babies found their way into the Etheric. So have fun—but do *not* take it too far." Bethany Anne swiped Michael's sword from the counter and made her way over to the door, where the men waited with barely-concealed impatience.

Jean nodded, dropping her eyes to hide the mischievous gleam. "I won't have *any* fun if you stand there giving me instructions all damned night. Go have a blast, and give 'em hell from me."

Above High Tortuga, QBS *ArchAngel II*, Bridge

Bethany Anne paced the bridge impatiently, then looked up at a representation of her own face on the screen. "ArchAngel, are they here yet?" She had been waiting for an eternity. Or so it felt when the night's activities called her.

Her hands clenched and unclenched, the energy coursing through her already annoying.

ArchAngel mirrored Bethany Anne's movements. "Almost, Mother. The transport Pod will arrive shortly."

She pressed her lips together. "Give me a feed to the Pod, please."

ArchAngel's screen split and showed the interior of the Pod. John, who had stayed behind to make sure the rest of the team caught up, and Darryl were asleep on their benches. Gabrielle and Tabitha were on the back bench with their heads together, talking quietly. Eric yawned and rolled first one shoulder, then the other to loosen them, while Scott snoozed on the bench across from him.

She cocked her head. "How can they be so relaxed?"

ArchAngel raised her eyebrows. "They have not been kept to the same level of confinement as you have been, Mother. Perhaps having a little time to stretch your legs will help you relax as well."

"True." She frowned at the screen, and then a smile touched the corner of her mouth. "Give me an audio feed into the Pod. Crank it up."

"Of course." ArchAngel matched Bethany Anne's playful smile with one of her own just as Michael entered the bridge.

Michael looked at the twin expressions of his wife and

her avatar and took a seat. "Whatever it is you two are planning..." His eyes flicked to the Pod feed. "Actually, no, never mind. Go ahead."

Bethany Anne blew him a kiss. "I knew there was a reason I married you."

Michael tilted his chin. "Besides my dashing looks, impeccable manners, nice ass, and rugged charm, you mean?" He moved to the seat next to hers. "So what nefarious prank do you have in mind, and what exactly did they do to deserve it?"

Bethany Anne encompassed the screen with a wave of her hand. "Look at them! I'm all fired up and ready to go, and *they're* all lounging around like a bunch of senior citizens after a potluck." She turned back to the screen. "HEY! This isn't the *Queen's Senior Citizen Bitches* on tour. *WAKE THE FUCK UP!*"

It had the desired effect. Mostly.

While everyone else almost jumped out of their skin at the sudden yell, John just opened one eye and glanced at the camera. "Hey, boss. I take it you're ready to get off-planet, then?"

Bethany Anne nodded. "You know it. Three years is a hell of a long time to be in one place. Now, you guys shake a damned leg and get your asses up here so we can get this party started."

Above Belv'th, QBS *ArchAngel II*

Tabitha looked down at the mudball and grimaced. "This place is a shithole. Three years on lockdown and you couldn't have brought us somewhere nice for our first night out? Fuck. I might as well have stayed in."

Scott murmured, "Yeah, there's not much down there, BA. Did we really need to bother with the armor?" He stuffed a hand down his shirt to adjust the plate that was bugging him. "I hate these sticky pads."

"Why is that?" Eric looked at his friend. "You get your chest hair caught again?"

"It's not funny," Scott grumped. He rubbed his chest.

"It could be worse," Bethany Anne told him. "You could have the damn thing stuck directly to your nipples. You don't even know pain until you take *that* shit off."

"You got that right," Tabitha agreed. She sat down and crossed her feet on the console. She used the wicked-looking blade she was holding to pare away the last piece of something that looked a little like an apple. "So, BA, are you gonna tell us why you brought us all the way out to the ass-end of nowhere? I don't even know what planet this is. What's this place called?" She popped the "apple" in her mouth and made a face when the tart juice hit her tongue.

"It hasn't got a name at the moment, although some call it 'Belv'th.'" Bethany Anne slapped Tabitha's feet down as she passed the console on her way to her chair. "ADAM gave me what he found, but this place values its privacy, so there wasn't much more than scan data to go off. What I *do* know is that it has a reputation in certain circles as being a place you can go to hide from the authorities."

Tabitha put her feet back up and wiped her knife on her pant leg before sheathing it again, ignoring Michael's raised eyebrow. "So it's like, what...Pirate Central? 'Cuz I never get tired of schooling *those* assholes."

Bethany Anne shook her head. "No, but they do have a

nasty infestation of the fuckers, and they cause the regular people no end of trouble. Most of the residents want to just be left alone to live their lives without interference."

John raised an eyebrow. "You mean without paying taxes."

She shrugged. "I can't argue; that might be a motivation for some." She waved at the planet on the screen. "Although you'd be surprised how many of them just want to be out from under government control. ArchAngel, open a map and highlight the main populated areas. Show topography, and use color to show population density in each sector."

A map of the planet appeared on the screen. There were two large cities, identifiable by the bullseye display of Bethany Anne's filters around each. The cities were splotches of midnight in the center, surrounded by rings of progressively paler blue. Bethany Anne pointed to the darkest spot on the map. "Okay, we have three main groups. The largest city is mostly the den of iniquity you'd expect to find at the center of the black market. It's full of shifty individuals with half their attention on their profit, the other half on how to get a slice of their neighbor's profit, and the last part trying to use said profit for drunken debauchery."

"Sounds a lot like High Tortuga when we first arrived," Darryl supplied. "What are we here for, then? To check it out?"

"Exactly." Bethany Anne tapped the finger against her lips. "I want to know if this place is actually decent, or if it's too out of control to meet our needs. Maybe we'll just have a fun night out, or maybe we're here to explore New Devon."

Michael tilted his head. "You think this," he pointed to the screen, "could be what we need for Phase Two?"

She tilted her hand left and right. "Like I said, maybe. It's the most likely candidate we've found so far. ADAM tells me that it's more like controlled anarchy than out-and-out lawlessness in the second city."

Darryl shifted around in his chair to scrutinize the map. "They're legit, then?"

Bethany Anne shrugged. "Kinda? Sort of." She paused for a moment. "Probably not. I expect some kind of criminal organization is running the show there."

Michael nodded toward the third highlighted area, which covered a wide, less-developed area that ran the length of an extensive lake system. It encompassed twice the area of the more densely populated cities. "What's the story with this location?" He pointed out a couple of mid-blue smears which stood out against the surrounding area.

Bethany Anne scratched her nose. "There are towns all along the lakes. Not sure what we'll find there, but by all accounts the townspeople make old Earth survivalists look like a weekend Scout jamboree. They take zero shit, and have fewer fucks to give than perhaps even you."

Tabitha grinned. "So what are we waiting for? Let's get our asses down there and start singing kumbaya with the anarchists."

Bethany Anne shook her head. "Michael and I will be taking the lake towns. Tabitha, you're with John and Scott. Go to the second city and find out what's going on there. Darryl, Eric, Gabrielle, same, but you three are hitting the big city."

Tabitha scowled. "What, so Mom and Dad get to go

play with the anarchists," she jerked a thumb toward Gabrielle, "big sis gets to stomp some pirate ass, and I get stuck with a boring-ass crime syndicate?"

"You can always stay here," Michael told her.

She rolled her eyes and headed for the door. "Whatever, Dad. I'll go get my shit."

Michael smiled as she walked out. He suspected that as soon as she was out of sight behind the door, she probably flipped him off for good measure.

He did like a challenge.

Three cloaked Pods peeled away from the *ArchAngel II* and slid into the planet's atmosphere.

"We all good?" Bethany Anne checked. "Everyone clear on what they're doing?"

"Go down, find bad-guys, have fun," came the response from Tabitha.

"Same here," Gabrielle replied.

"See you all in a few hours." She clicked off the connection and turned to her husband. "So...we are all alone, at last."

"I still don't see why we're heading for the outlying towns," Michael grumped. Bethany Anne frowned at him in disbelief. Michael matched her frown with one of his own. "All of the pirates will be attracted to the major cities. You *promised* me pirates."

Was that almost a pout? Bethany Anne kept her amusement off her face.

There was no fucking way she would ever admit that

she found her husband's sulking just a tiny bit adorable. "We're going there because this section requires finesse, and I thought you'd enjoy a challenge." She shrugged, unconcerned. "We can go back and chase down assholes with the others if you'd like." She patted his arm when he shook his head. "Besides, even if nothing serious goes down out there, I'm sure you'll get to burn off energy somehow. This whole planet is just crawling with shit-heads in need of an education."

"Hmmm…" Michael laced his hands together, his brow furrowed in thought. "Okay, I suppose we *might* have the better assignment. Tell me what you have in mind."

Bethany Anne winked and got up to go to the back. She returned a minute or two later carrying the box Jean had given her, set it down between them, and lifted the cover.

Michael's eyebrows came together in surprise. "Is that…"

Bethany Anne smiled. "It is."

CHAPTER FOUR

Belv'th, Second City, Entertainment District

Tabitha pushed open the door of the bar as though it had offended her in some way.

Scott watched her go in with a wary look before whispering to John, "What crawled up her ass?"

John shrugged and followed her into the bar. It was hot, and crowded with people from a mix of species. He pointed Tabitha out, and they worked through the crowd to where she had claimed a stool at the bar.

She drummed her fingers on the polished wood. "This place better have something edible."

John stared at the occupant of the stool to her right and sat down beside her when they picked up their drink and moved on with a grumble.

"I didn't think it was possible, but you're even perkier than usual," Scott teased as he took the one to her left. He bumped her shoulder with his. "What's the problem?"

"My problem," Tabitha ground out, "is that I'm here on

date night without my *Gott Verdammt* date." She signaled the bartender with a wiggle of her fingers.

"Yeah, you and me both," Scott commiserated.

Tabitha raised an eyebrow. "Yeah, but trawling for a bar fight isn't exactly the kind of night you and Cheryl Lynn would choose as a couples activity. Nothing adds a little spice to the evening activities than getting all sweaty beforehand." She turned to the other side. "John knows what I mean, don't you?" She dug an elbow into John's side.

John smiled.

The Torcellan bartender made her way over and looked them up and down. "Oh, joy. Humans. I'll warn you now that you'll pay for any damages you cause." Her disapproving frown melted away when they nodded, and she was all smiles. "Now, what can I get you?"

"Do you have a menu?" Tabitha asked.

The bartender reached under the bar and produced three menus. "Drinks?"

John grunted. "You got Coke?"

The Torcellan shook her head.

"Pepsi?" Scott asked.

She shook her head again. "No, we don't trade in Federation goods around here. Local producers only."

Tabitha looked up from the menu and tilted her head at the bartender. "Well, what *do* you have? Something that goes with…" She held the menu and pointed at an image of something that looked a little like a burger. The bun was red, but so was the meat and that suited her just fine.

She turned around and came back with three bottles. "Try this."

Tabitha took one look at the familiar label and tried not to grin. "This will do, thanks." Tabitha took a big swig and then, eyes open, turned to look at her companions before belching. She sent her thoughts directly to John and Scott. *Let's not tell her this came from a less-than-independent brewery.*

All right with me, John agreed. *Especially if this place ends up being the new Devon. Hey, Scott, maybe you can get Cheryl Lynn to set up an AGB here. This place hasn't exactly rolled out the welcome mat.*

Tabitha snorted, spraying the bar in front of her with beer. The bartender looked at her and lifted an eyebrow.

Tabitha glared at her. "Yes?"

John put a hand on her arm. "Easy, wildcat." He turned to the bartender, who had taken a step back. "Sorry about her. She gets cranky when she hasn't eaten."

And you can kiss my bodacious ass, Tabitha told him sweetly.

John ignored her. He gathered the menus and handed them back to the bartender. "We'll all have the same."

"And another round," Scott added as he put his empty bottle down on the bar.

Getting up after they got their new drinks, they walked over to a table at the back with a beer in each hand and chatted until their food was brought to them by a waiter. The food on the plate looked a lot less appetizing than the picture on the menu had.

Tabitha picked her not-burger up and inhaled suspiciously. "Smells good, so I don't need to care what it *looks* like..." She screwed her face up and took a bite, and her eyes popped as she chewed. "Oh, my...mffff." She put the burger down and chewed with her eyes closed. "Ohhh, that's good."

She looked at John and Scott, who were watching her more than a little doubtfully. She pointed at their untouched food with her free hand. "You guys, eat the fucking burger, or *I'm* gonna." She picked hers up and took another monster bite. "Sheershly, shh goog."

John and Scott exchanged a shrug and grabbed their food. "Here goes nothing," John murmured. His eyes declared his surprise that for once, or at least once recently, Tabitha wasn't trying to surprise him.

Tabitha finished her last bite and wiped her fingers on her napkin. "So now we've eaten. Where do you guys wanna start looking?"

An angry voice from near the bar answered the question for them. They looked over to where a Shrillexian running his mouth sat at the end of the bar with a Noel-ni, a Baka, and two more Shrillexians.

"You can't go anywhere on the planet these days without a bunch of humans showing up," the speaker continued his tirade. "Damn vermin foul up every raid we plan. *Can't* take slaves, *can't* raid the mines for profit, *can't* even keep what's rightfully ours when we earned it through honest brute force. Not with the humans around. What are we going to do?"

The Noel-ni to his left shrugged, her lips drawn back in anger. "I dunno. All I know is that I signed onto this crew with the promise of much profit, and all our profit was taken back by the damned humans."

The Shrillexian took a sip of his beer. Tabitha couldn't figure out if his grimace was for the drink or the conversation. "How," one of the Shrillexians asked, "is a mercenary supposed to profit?"

The loudmouth's opinion was not unpopular. His companions cheered his vitriol, egging him on. "Melien is right. We don't have to put up with this shit. He's got a plan to get them gone. Did you hear him speak? He says the Federation is weak without their Bitch leading them, so we should cleanse this planet of humans once and for all. Take it back for ourselves."

John's easy grin faded. *I believe we have our first contenders.*

Just how many humans are here? Scott wondered. *Sure sounds like they've been giving these assholes a hard time.*

Tabitha tossed her napkin on the table and started to stand, but John gave her a minute shake of his head. *Just wait. They're part of a bigger group. We'll follow them back, find this Melien, and take out the whole nest.*

Tabitha stuck her tongue out at him but sat back down.

The Shrillexian banged his glass down on the bar and pushed his stool away with a loud scrape, startling the Torcellan barmaid. "I say we listen to Melien. We'll take them out while they sleep. Who here is with me?"

The mercenaries in his group were with him. Then again, he'd been buying the drinks during the night.

The crew headed for the door in an undisciplined scramble.

Tabitha reached into the inside breast pocket of her coat and brought out three small spheres. She tossed them into the air in the general direction of the door and they took flight, trained in on the Shrillexian and his band of merry maladjusted.

The Noel-ni in the group spotted the hovering spheres and scanned the bar. When her eyes alighted on Tabitha she shrugged, then gave a shit-eating grin and flipped her off.

"Humans!" she hissed to her group.

Dammit, Tabbie! John growled and stood. *We were supposed to let them get back to the leader.*

The Shrillexian halted, his back to them. His fists clenched and unclenched a couple of times, and he spun to face them. His nostrils flared as he pushed a couple of chairs out of the way.

Then he charged.

Belv'th, Town on the Lakes, Salt Mine

K'aia tucked her back legs underneath her and tried to make herself as small as possible. Not an easy feat for a four-legged Yollin, and even less simple with the added bulk of the human body she was carrying. However, since the crack in the rocks was the only place she could find to hide from the guards, she did the best she could with what she had until they had passed and she could escape the mine.

She hadn't been born a slave. She'd been stolen from her home farther along the coast and brought here to work in the salt mines. The work wasn't difficult. In fact, she found it strangely cathartic to spend her days thinking while she chipped away at the salt deposits.

Hell, she even did extra so the weaker ones could get a break from the overseers. They didn't care as long as the carts were filled just as fast, and she didn't mind the labor. It was just her way.

She'd toiled without complaint for years beyond counting, but no longer.

She looked down at the bundle in her arms. Today the overseer had used the electro-whip on Barien, her only friend in this Empress-forsaken place. Barien had collapsed on the spot, his frail human body unable to take the voltage designed for much sturdier species, such as her own.

Her friend's death had caused something in K'aia to snap. She was meek by nature, and until today had been biddable and easy to control, much to her shame. But seeing Barien's twitching corpse had broken her.

And it was for the better.

The overseer was dead now. K'aia had dashed over and snatched the lash out of the slave driver's hand, and used it to scour the skin from his body. She'd shocked her slave collar with the tip of the lash to short the lock, disregarding the pain it caused, before wrapping Barien's rapidly-cooling body in a tarp and running for her life.

K'aia knew if she could reach the human town then she would be safe. It was very well defended, and if she knew anything about humans, the people would take care of her friend's funeral even though they weren't related by blood. Then she would go and find her own people, if any remained.

All she had to do was make it out of the mine.

The bootsteps faded and K'aia risked a glance from her hiding place. The guards were gone. She reaffirmed her hold on Barien's body and broke her cover.

Bethany Anne and Michael walked hand-in-hand along the sand between the lake shore and the cliff, heading for the town in the near distance. Bethany Anne let go of Michael's hand and slipped her arm through his. "It's not quite the barefoot stroll under the stars I'd imagined, but it is rather pretty here."

Michael glanced at a construction on the cliff face up ahead, which looked to be the entrance to a mine. His nose wrinkled. "If you don't mind the smell of salt."

She smiled. "Nothing's perfect." They walked a ways farther before she spoke again. "It's damn close, though. What do you—" She was interrupted by the sight of a four-legged Yollin running out of the mine. "What the…"

The Yollin galloped toward them at breakneck speed, only barely hanging onto what looked suspiciously like a wrapped corpse.

Her mandibles clicked furiously, and her carapace heaved with the effort of trying to breathe. "Humans, run! They will take you! Oh, bistok shit, you *can't* understand me!"

Bethany Anne held up a hand. "We understand you just fine. Who is 'they,' who are you, and why are you carrying…" she sniffed as they came closer. "A *dead* human?"

The Yollin looked from Bethany Anne to Michael and back again. Her mandibles fell open in pure shock. "My Empress!" She bent awkwardly.

Bethany Anne waved her off. "Didn't you hear? I'm not an empress anymore, thank fuck, and that bowing shit got old fast."

The Yollin straightened. "I'm sorry, my Empress. I am K'aia, and this was my friend Barien. We were slaves, but I killed the overseer for killing Barien and escaped."

Bethany Anne's lip curled. "Slaves?" Her face darkened, and the color bled from her hair even as her teeth became suddenly much sharper.

K'aia took an involuntary step back at the sight of the Witch.

"My love." Michael's voice interrupted K'aia's jumbled clicks.

Baba Yaga turned red eyes on Michael, who was gazing at the two score guards who had piled out of the mine entrance while they were talking with a gleam in his eyes.

She narrowed her eyes at the guards, her hands on her gun belt. She let out a throaty chuckle. "You see, my love? I told you we'd get a chance to let off a little steam."

Michael made a sweeping gesture toward the guards. "After you, my love."

K'aia wondered what she had stumbled into.

Belv'th, First City, Bazaar

Gabrielle, Eric, and Darryl walked under the covered arch into a rainbow of the neon lights. They were immediately assaulted by a million smells, colors, and sounds.

The people, a mix of species they knew and some they didn't, pressed up against each other as they navigated the twisting paths between the stalls squeezed into every available space.

Darryl stared around in awe. "What the fuck is this place?"

Gabrielle smiled. "I remember markets like this back on Earth. Just follow my lead, and you'll be fine. And make sure you're actively repelling pickpockets."

The crowd parted around her as she sashayed over to the nearest food vendor and began the delicate process of haggling for their dinner. She returned a few minutes later with three wrapped packages, which she shared.

Eric peeled the wrapper back. "What've we got?"

"No idea. I just bought what the guy in front of me had." She shrugged, opened the wrapper, and sniffed. "Smells a little like a taco? Although if the street vendors here are like the ones I remember back on Earth, we might be glad of our nanocytes after eating them."

They walked through the bazaar, keeping their eyes and ears peeled for suspicious activity. Eric threw his wrapper in a trashcan as he passed.

Gabrielle huffed. "How are we supposed to find the criminals here? Everyone whose mind I've read is here on some shady business or other. They are *all* criminals. The question is merely one of degree."

Darryl nodded toward a rundown building. "What about there?" There was no signage to indicate what type of business it was. The windows were painted over, and the people around the doorway all had their faces covered.

Eric started for the building, calling over his shoulder, "You two coming, or are you gonna stand around talking about it all day?"

Gabrielle pulled her scarf up over her mouth. She shrugged at the look the Bitches gave her. "What? We want to blend in."

They entered the building behind a group of nervous-smelling Torcellans who seemed out of place. The brightness and anonymity of the open market were instantly replaced by ambient lighting—wildly-colored in-your-face lighting.

Gabrielle smirked as a deep bass pulse sent a frisson of electricity to the pit of her stomach. "It's a *nightclub?*"

Darryl grinned. "Well, Bethany Anne *did* say we had to explore. We wouldn't want to do half a job."

She clapped delightedly. "Exactly. And if there just happens to be a dance floor in our way, it would be rude *not* to follow the local customs while we are working." She grabbed Eric's hand and dragged him to the admissions desk, where an Ixtali took their entry fee and pressed a stamp to each of their hands.

They pushed through the heavy curtain to the main room beyond. It wasn't *quite* the kind of nightclub they'd expected.

The ambiance of the lobby was replaced by almost total darkness. The only light came from the backlit podiums scattered throughout the room, and the roaming strobes that danced over the darkness.

Gabrielle drew a breath when two beams crossed in front of her, throwing a low couch into relief—as well as the knot of writhing, sweaty bodies upon it.

Eric spoke into his wife's mind. *You sure you wanna join in with the local customs?*

She responded to his teasing with a soft sigh. *Been there, done that. Perhaps in France, but I'm not admitting anything. Come on, boys. I've found someone we should talk to.*

She slipped into the crowd, leaving Eric and Darryl to pick their jaws up from the floor.

Belv'th, Town on the Lakes, Salt Mine

The guards bunched in a half-circle about twenty feet away from the three of them. Neither human appeared the least bit fazed by the multitude of guards surrounding them with their electro-whips raised. In fact, if K'aia didn't know better, she'd say they were equal parts pissed and excited by the violence the situation promised.

The mine owner, a Leath, stood behind his men and shouted over their heads, "Drop your weapons and surrender my Yollin, and I'll let you go."

Baba Yaga tilted her head and gave him a sharp grin over the top of the Jean Dukes Special in her right hand. "How about you drop yours, and I won't kill every last motherfucking one of you slowly?"

You're going to let them live?

Her laugh tickled the back of Michael's mind. *Like fuck. They're all going to die horribly, although maybe not slowly, and then we're going to free the rest of the slaves.*

What about our young friend?

I have a feeling she will be eager to help out. She spoke into the Yollin's mind. *K'aia, do you feel like getting a little payback?*

K'aia's mandibles clicked rapidly in surprise. Of course, she had heard the legends and the rumors, but to be here and fight side-by-side with *her*?

She had never felt more *Yollin*.

She nodded at Baba Yaga and stepped away to place Barien's body down reverently beside a tree, then moved to back up Baba Yaga and her consort.

Six guards stepped forward at an order from the mine owner.

Baba Yaga shook a finger at them. "Nuh-uh. Stay right where you are." They didn't, so she shot them as soon as they took the first step.

"What am I paying you for?" the Leath screamed in anger, pointing. "Get them, you fools!"

The guards surged forward.

Before K'aia had even dispatched the Zhyn who came at her, Baba Yaga had worked her way through them in a storm of kinetics and claws. A few made a break for the mine entrance, but one by one they jerked and fell as Michael calmly picked them off.

K'aia knocked away a Skaine with her bony elbow, then slashed him with the electro-whip she tore from his hand. "I hope you have no afterlife!" She crushed his head with her front foot and moved on to the next.

Baba Yaga opened a throat with her claws and stepped over the fallen body to get to the Leath, who was backing up with terror stamped across his features.

He slipped on the entrails of one of his ex-guards, landing heavily on his ass. He scrabbled backward with his feet, pointing at Baba Yaga with a shaky hand. "You have no power here! You can't come into my place of business and start killing indiscriminately!"

Baba Yaga stalked over to him and picked him up by his thick neck. He struggled, trying to pull her fingers apart as he kicked the air.

She made a face as she felt his veins throb under her hand. "Who said it was *indiscriminate?*" She ended the conversation with a squeeze and dropped the dead Leath to the ground with a look of disgust. "I'm not even going to bury scum like that."

She held her hands up and concentrated for a second, and her hands were clean again. She ran them through her hair, and when she looked up again, the Witch was gone. Bethany Anne rolled her shoulders and stretched, then looked at Michael and K'aia. "I suppose that will do as a warmup."

Michael shook his head at the ring of corpses around them. "They never listen, do they?"

Bethany Anne grinned as she holstered her pistol. "Is utter obedience from scum-sucking bottom-dwellers too much to ask for?"

CHAPTER FIVE

Belv'th, Second City

"DRAG'TAH HUMANS!"

The whole bar was in an uproar. The fight had quickly been taken up by the rest of the customers, and the bartender had crouched behind the bar to escape the furniture that was being thrown around.

John sidestepped a clumsy swipe and threw a monster right hook that knocked the Baka halfway across the floor. Its progress was stalled by the fixed table it crashed into.

It got up and roared mournfully at John, who couldn't believe his ears. He pointed to it. "Shit, they even *sound* like Wookies!"

"It almost feels wrong punching them," Scott called. He was holding the snapping Noel-ni away with one hand on the top of her head while he kicked a Skaine in the face. "I *hate* fighting the cute ones."

"I'm not having any issues," Tabitha snarked from the top of the bar. She smashed the stool she was holding into the face of the Shrillexian who'd started it all. He stumbled back but lunged again—straight into her boot. She dived onto his back and wrapped both arms around his neck.

Her voice cut through the noise in the bar. "Rodeo time, *bitches! Whooooot!*" The Shrillexian bucked to get her off, but Tabitha just clung tighter and rode him like a mechanical bull, all the while punching him in the head. "These fuckers always take a licking!"

The Baka roared again and charged John with a broken bottle in each hand. "Tabitha, stop jacking around." He blocked the Baka's downward swing and jabbed his shaggy attacker in the groin. The Baka folded, and John used the opportunity to grab the Baka's head and introduce its face to his knee.

He glanced down to make sure the creature stayed down this time.

John looked around to check on Scott, who was still trying to extricate himself from the Noel-ni. He held her at arm's length to avoid the whirlwind of claws. "Shit," he told her, "I'm sorry I suggested you get a rabies shot, okay? You're clearly just deranged."

She snarled and snapped at him. "I'll tear your face off and eat your eyeballs, human!"

Tabitha jumped off the bleeding Shrillexian on the floor. "Just hit her, already!" She bent to snatch a rifle twice the size of her arm from the Shrillexian's unconscious body.

Scott grimaced. "But she's so cute, even with all the 'grrrr.' Feels like I'd be kicking a panda or something. S'just *wrong.*"

Tabitha marched over and laid the Noel-ni out with a

jab to the back of her head from the butt of her new rifle. The Noel-ni's eyes rolled up, and she dropped. "There, problem solved." Tabitha made sure no one was on her six before turning back to Scott. "And I'll make sure to tell everyone that I had to save your ass from the cute, fluffy alien."

A Skaine came flying over their heads. "Duck!"

"You're supposed to yell *before* you throw," Tabitha bitched. She grabbed a two-legged Yollin coming at her and flung him into the optics display behind the bar.

"You're paying for that!" they heard the bartender yell over the falling glass. A pale, slender hand reached up and plucked the one remaining bottle from the shelf. "*All* of it!"

Tabitha and Scott turned to grin at John as the patrons of the bar gathered in a loose circle around them. Scott made a face of mock-horror at the weapons that appeared in their hands. "Looks like playtime's over. They have *guns*."

John frowned at the would-be assailants. "Those aren't *guns*." He held up the pistols made by his wife. "*These* are guns."

Tabitha cracked up, almost getting hit by a Skaine in her abandon. She sidestepped and kicked the Skaine away. "I can't believe you even did that," she managed through her laughter.

John's eyes blazed red. "Now, I'm gonna count to five, and then it's gonna suck to be anyone still standing here."

He pulled the hammers back (which, on a Jean Dukes pistol were completely for show, but Jean liked to make her husband happy.) "*One…*"

Belv'th, Town on the Lakes, Irey

K'aia was going to return to the mine and help them organize it into something that could support the workers for the foreseeable future.

However, she had something important to do first.

She had refused all offers of help with Barien's body. While Bethany Anne had gone into the mine to release all the workers and Michael had been searching the offices, she had taken his body to the baths and cleaned and wrapped it in a richly embroidered cloth she'd taken from the wall outside the dead mine owner's office.

Barien made his final journey in her arms, flanked on either side by the most powerful honor guard she could possibly have asked for.

When they reached Irey, a mercenary outpost, a soldier leaned over the wall and told them to fuck off. "Whatever you're sellin', we don't want it."

Bethany Anne frowned at him. "Do I *look* like a fucking salesperson? Open up, or you won't have a gate left to open."

The soldier squinted to see her face. "Oh shit."

A few minutes later the gate was opened just a crack by a man with a rifle in a crumpled military-style jacket over what was clearly nightwear. He blinked owlishly at them. "Oh, shit. I mean, you're the fucking *Empress*."

"I told you, Gerry," the guard piped up from behind him

Michael snickered. "No introductions are necessary, then."

The man glared at them. "We don't want your kind here. We rule ourselves."

"'Our kind?'" Bethany Anne rolled her eyes. "Just let us in. It's already been a long night."

Gerry looked at K'aia. "A Yollin? What's that you're carrying?"

Bethany Anne translated for K'aia, who stepped forward holding her friend. "This is Barien. He was killed. I brought him here to be sent on to his afterlife according to the ways of your people."

The hostility faded from Gerry's face. He lowered his rifle, stepped back, and opened the gate. "I suppose you'd better come in then."

"About time." Bethany Anne marched past him. "Oh, and you can probably expect a few more people. The salt mine has gone out of business." She looked back at K'aia. "The previous owner got called away." Bethany Anne strode a few more steps before adding, "To the afterlife."

Gerry led Bethany Anne, Michael, and K'aia to a long, low building constructed from roughly cut stones. "Go on in. I'm going to find someone to help your friend there." He pointed at K'aia. "I need to get back to my beauty sleep."

"Who's in charge here?" Bethany Anne asked.

Gerry laughed. "In charge? Oh, that's just…" He walked off, clutching a hand to his stomach. "Someone will be with you soon."

Bethany Anne looked at Michael, who shrugged and walked inside the building. She waved K'aia in and followed behind.

Belv'th, First City, Bazaar

Gabrielle and Darryl waited by the fountain in the open

square. The cool night breeze was a relief after the thick air and close quarters inside the club.

Eric appeared from a gap in the crowd, carrying three takeout cups. "Hey, it's not coffee, but you were right. It's damn close!"

Gabrielle took hers and sipped it gratefully. "Mmmm, nutty. We have to get some of this to take back to High Tortuga." She looked up at the ships cutting through the traffic lanes above. "You know, I kind of like this place."

"How so?" Darryl asked.

She smirked. "It has an edge to it. Look up there." She indicated the ships slicing through the atmosphere above them. "The energy coming from most of these people is incredible. They feel free, and they're proud and happy. They work hard and play harder. What's not to like?"

"Most?" Eric hadn't missed his wife's qualifier.

Gabrielle wrinkled her nose. "Yes, well. We can take care of *them*. I think this place is..." She trailed off as her eyes wandered to a commotion on the other side of the square.

She stood to get a better look. The flurry of movement came from a hastily-erected stage, where a heavily scarred Baka duked it out with a nine-foot lizard-looking alien to cheers from the crowd.

Gabrielle's eyes lit up. "Guys, is that... Are they *prize-fighting*?"

Belv'th, Town on the Lakes

They left K'aia at the gates and headed back along the shoreline. Michael had found evidence in the mine owner's office that pointed back to a mercenary company based in the first city.

"I can't believe how they run things there. It is not even a city. Isolated communities, no infrastructure other than what anyone is willing to provide for a price. Gerry told me that they don't even have any administration for local matters, no law, and no responsibility for anything other than themselves and their dependents."

Bethany Anne shrugged. "Yeah, well. If it works for them, then I suppose they don't need to define their roles too much. Who are we to judge?"

"How can they survive with so little structure?" Michael grumped. "I can't believe it works."

She didn't try to hide her amusement. "You wanted to tell them to make a damn decision, didn't you? Please tell me it wasn't just me they drove batshit with their endless debate?"

He smirked, then sighed. "So damn much. From what I gather, that's pretty much the system around these parts. I refrained from laughing and asking how *no* system could be a system, but only just."

Bethany Anne squeezed his hand. "That's progress. I remember a time when you would have just ripped their heads off and installed leaders who did things your way."

The memory that came unbidden brought a small smile to his lips. "Those were the days. Be that as it may, I have made more than a little effort to 'chill out,' as everybody keeps saying."

"Don't think I haven't noticed," she told him. "I like this softer side of you. Our children couldn't have a better father than the man you're becoming."

He looked away. "Don't think I haven't noticed that you are much more willing to spill blood since I left you for a while."

She arched an eyebrow. "You say it like that's a bad thing."

"Not necessarily." He sniffed. "Can you smell that?"

Bethany Anne scented the air. "Salt...and smoke." She looked into the distance, seeing a small town some way along the shore. "Shit, we'd better go and see if they need help."

Michael was already speeding toward their goal. "Race you," he called back.

"Oh, it's on."

Their humor was lost when they reached the town and all that remained was a blackened ruin. Michael caught up to Bethany Anne at the town limit, where she stood looking out at the devastation in simmering silence.

He took her hand. "There may be survivors."

She shook her head. "There's nobody here. This isn't fresh."

"We should search anyway."

"We'll split up and search quickly, then get back to the *ArchAngel* and figure out which fuckers did this." Her face worked through her emotions, finally settling on a cold mask. "This is the downside to the anarchy the people of that city love so much. They have ultimate freedom, but no Justice. I can see why ADAM picked this place."

Michael scrutinized her for a moment, then nodded and slipped into the shadows.

Bethany Anne walked in the opposite direction, her

anger rising with every step she took. Who had done this to these people?

By all accounts, they were the misfits; outcasts on a planet full of them. Still, they deserved better than whatever happened here.

Everywhere she looked were signs of a struggle. The odd corpse here and there told her everything she needed to know. A twisted corpse in a melted mercenary uniform lay in the doorway of one of the burnt houses.

She walked on. A Noel-ni stared sightlessly from the mouth of an alley. When she bent to examine the corpse, she recognized the telltale scorch marks from an electro-whip on its matted fur. Closer inspection revealed manacle scarring on the body's wrists and ankles.

More fucking slavery.

She summoned the Pod and turned on her heel to storm back toward the edge of town. **Michael, we're getting out of here. Looks like those basic assholes need our attention, after all.**

Belv'th, First City, Bazaar

Darryl stuck his fingers in his mouth and whistled.

"Go, baby!" Gabrielle jumped up and down on the spot. Her cheeks were pink, and her scarf had fallen away.

Eric flashed them a quick grin and ducked the claws coming at his throat. He used the momentum to drop and sweep his opponent's legs. Unfortunately for Eric, this species had backward-facing knee joints.

He rolled out of the way just before it landed on top of

him and flipped to his feet. His opponent got up and squared up to Eric again.

The fight was drawing a substantial crowd. Gabrielle and Darryl were surrounded by baying spectators, most with their heads and faces covered for anonymity.

"Who *are* these people?" one hooded figure asked another. "They're not like any humans I've ever met."

"And do you see that female?" the other asked. "I'd pay good currency for the use of her."

Eric was suddenly gone from the stage. Gabrielle spun to find him. Darryl chuckled and pointed to the other side of the stage. "Oh shit, now they've done it."

The figure who'd spoken second was now hanging in the air, suspended by the throat from Eric's hand. The crowd didn't care who was fighting or where, as long as there was a fight to watch. They shifted to reform the circle around Eric.

Eric's eyes narrowed. "That's my wife you just disrespected." His friend found himself in a similar situation in Eric's other hand. He gave them both a shake that rattled their brains in their skulls and held them out to face Gabrielle. He ground the words out from between clenched teeth. "Apologize to her. *Now.*"

Their eyes bulged out from under their hoods. Both gasped and scratched uselessly at the constraint against their continued ability to breathe. They were saved from what came next by Bethany Anne, although they would never know it.

Shit, I should have come up with call signs or something. Gabrielle, we're on our way to you. We found a mine full of

slaves and links to a mercenary group in the city that supplied them. Baba Yaga is just itching to meet them.

Shit. Darryl snickered. He looked around at the many uniforms scattered among the crowd. *Wait until you get here. Every fucking one of them is either a merc or a criminal.*

What have you found?

Eric dropped the two assholes with a grimace, and they pushed through the grumbling crowd. *We found exactly what we expected. It's Crime Central here.*

It's only a crime if there's a law to forbid it, Gabrielle pointed out.

You were always the more diplomatic one, Bethany Anne replied.

Gabrielle sniffed. *The place is definitely full of duplicitous assholes, though. I've been reading minds the whole time, and there are a number of less than salubrious characters we should take a closer look at.*

What was out by the lakes? Eric asked.

Mostly the slaves. They're free now. We also had the enlightening experience of visiting one of the merc towns out there. They're mostly decent people. Rough and totally batshit, but honest enough. Have you picked up any rumors of slavery in the city?

Gabrielle frowned. *No, just a thriving sex trade.*

I'd better not find the two are connected, or there won't be a planet left to clean up.

Gabrielle smiled. *Didn't seem that way from what we saw.*

Yeah, Darryl chipped in. *We ended up in some kind of sex den. They all looked more than happy to be there.*

What about the second city? What did they find there? Eric asked before Bethany Anne could press them for more details.

Michael answered. *More mercenaries and plenty of anti-human sentiment.*

Bethany Anne chuckled. **It seems that a few of the humans in the second city have taken it upon themselves to fuck things up for the slavers.**

Gabrielle grinned. *My kind of people.*

You've got that right. Look sharp, we're here.

The Pod landed, and Bethany Anne and Michael got out. Two minutes later the third Pod arrived.

Tabitha swaggered down the ramp with a scowl on her face and a big-ass rifle resting on her shoulder.

Darryl burst out laughing.

Tabitha tilted her chin defiantly. "What?"

"You look like…" Darryl froze when Tabitha turned a hard stare on him.

"Next words out of your mouth should be along the lines of 'a complete badass and every red-blooded male's wet dream,' or you're going to be getting intimate with my new friend Gracie here." She dropped the rifle to her hip for emphasis. "How does Natalia feel about you seeing other women?"

Darryl opened his mouth to speak.

"Save it," Bethany Anne told Tabitha. "We have work to do." She turned to Michael. **Next time we bring her boy toy along with us.**

"What's the plan, boss?" John asked.

Bethany Anne's smile fell short of her eyes. "I got with ArchAngel and ADAM on the way over here. We have the locations of three merc companies in this city that are definitely involved in the slave trade, and several that have links to the first three. How involved they are is unclear, so we'll focus on the big ones. And by 'focus,' I mean *terminate the fuckers with extreme prejudice.*"

Scott frowned. "What about the rest of it? The fights, the sex trade, and the crime?"

Bethany Anne shrugged. "Not our problem. If they want to live like this, I'm not too bothered about it. It suits what I had in mind, anyway."

"You've settled on this place, then?" Michael asked.

Bethany Anne grinned and spread her arms wide. "Welcome to New Devon."

CHAPTER SIX

New Devon, First City, Mercenary Compound #1

The Pod hung in the air above the mercenary compound. Bethany Anne studied the heat signatures on the screen. "Looks like they're mostly concentrated on the ground floor like the fucking roaches they are."

Michael made a face. "Hardly a challenge."

Bethany Anne rolled her eyes. "Has everyone got their comm in?"

Tabitha answered in their ears, "If it's a challenge you wanted, then you two should have picked this place."

Michael leaned over and pressed the button to open a video link to Tabitha. Her face appeared in a window on the screen. "What have you got there?" he asked.

She did something, and her face was replaced with a feed of the compound below the Pod. "Mine's bigger than yours," she teased.

Her teasing was cut off by Scott's voice. "We're in position. Ready on your go, BA."

"Bethany Anne isn't here to take your call right now," Baba Yaga snarked. "Now let's go fuck up some pirates!"

"Mercenaries," Michael corrected.

She flashed sharp teeth at him. "What-the-fuck-*ever*. They all bleed the same, don't they?"

Michael turned off the video. "That they do, my love. That they do."

High Tortuga, Space Fleet Base, Nursery

Alexis woke from a dream about her mother. Rubbing her eyes, she sat up inside the Pod-crib and brushed her hand on the light sensor. "Phyrro, where is Mommy?"

The twins' EI appeared on the small screen beside her head. "Your mother is still on her date. Would you like me to tell Aunt Jean you are awake?"

Alexis shook her head and scooted to the edge of her bed. "No, thank you, Phyrro." She wrapped her blanket around her shoulders and opened the Pod. *Gabriel, wake up.*

I'm already awake, he replied. His Pod opened and he sat up in his bed, rubbing his eyes like she had. *Why are we awake?*

Alexis shooed him over and got onto the bed beside him. "I had a dream that Mommy was fighting with some bad guys."

Gabriel put his arm around his sister, who was shaking a little from the residue of the dream. *Show me.*

Alexis shared the scattered images from her dream.

Gabriel's eyes grew wide. *That doesn't look like a dream.* "Phyrro, where are Mommy and Daddy?"

"They are still on their date, as I told Alexis."

"Are they safe?"

A micro-pause. "They are."

Gabriel's nose scrunched in thought. "Can you show us where they are?"

"I'm not sure," the EI admitted. "One moment."

In the living quarters, Jean was getting up close and personal with a pint of triple chocolate something-or-other ice-cream and the specs for a device she was considering installing in her lab when the twins' EI pinged her. "What's up, Phyrro?"

Phyrro's avatar came up on her tablet. "The children are asking to be shown where their parents are."

Jean furrowed her brow. "What's the problem?"

"This." Phyrro's face was replaced with a feed to wherever the hell Bethany Anne was. The Queen wore Baba Yaga's face, and she was in the middle of delivering a serious ass-kicking.

Jean snickered and pointed her spoon at the video, a glint of amusement in her eyes. "You can show them."

"I certainly will *not* show them that," Phyrro argued. "My duty is to protect them from harm, not scar them psychologically."

Jean stuck the spoon in her mouth. "Whath's the harm in thowing them their parents can protecth them—and othersth—when it comes down to ith?"

Baba Yaga beheaded three mercenaries on the screen, and let rip a string of expletives as the blood sprayed her. Phyrro's face reappeared, judging Jean.

She shook her head, biting back a smirk as she twirled her spoon in a "go on" motion. "Okay, okay. You can time-delay the feed and cut out the gory bits. But let them see the strength they were born to."

Phyrro sounded pretty uncertain for an EI. "If you say so."

"I do," Jean stated.

Phyrro cut the connection, and Jean got back to her manual. The smirk she'd hidden appeared at the corner of her mouth. It was the smirk of a mother who was finally getting her own back on a family member who'd been a pain in her parenting experience.

New Devon, First City, Mercenary Compound Number Three

Gabrielle frowned as she looked up and behind her head. "There's nobody here. This place is *creepy*."

Michael's surprise came through on the comm. "Is it abandoned?"

"It doesn't look like it," Gabrielle confirmed. "Although...if they were out on a contract, it would explain why this place is locked down. We're going to do a quick search, then we'll head on over to you."

"No," he told her. "Get over to the other location once you've got their data. We're going that way too once we're done here."

"Got you." Gabrielle turned to Darryl and Eric. "You heard the man. Let's move."

They worked through the lower level, clearing each room as they passed it on their way to what had to be the administration offices.

"What are we looking for?" Darryl asked when they were inside.

She opened a filing cabinet and began to rifle the contents. "Names? Accounts? Anything that points to where we can find the slaves the bastards took. Anything that tells us where they are now."

Eric laid a brief hand on her shoulder as he walked past. "We'll find them. We'll find them, and we'll make them pay."

She looked at him with hard, too-bright eyes. "Too fucking right we will."

Darryl called from a side room he'd gone to explore. "I got the boss's office over here. EI says the guy's name is...*Melien.*" Darryl's head popped through the doorway, one eyebrow raised. "Didn't the dick John's team got into a fight with mention that name?" he asked before his head disappeared once more.

Gabrielle and Eric made their way to the office and Darryl waved them over to the computer he was sitting at. "This guy is exactly the kind of fuckface who needs to stop wasting this planet's oxygen." He pulled up a file. "Or anyone's oxygen, really. Damn, look at this."

Gabrielle's voice growled low in her throat, and her lips drew back in a snarl. "These are *people*, and they're listed like...like *commodities*!" Her lips pressed together. "That's it! This bastard is going to die. Tonight."

She opened the link to Bethany Anne as she stalked out of the office. "BA, we've got the ringleader's name."

"Do you have the leader?" Baba Yaga asked.

"No, but I know where he'll be very shortly," Darryl cut

in. "There's a message from the asshole at Location Two calling for help."

"What's your status, Location Two?" Baba Yaga demanded.

Tabitha came back almost instantly, and the link was filled with the sounds of weapons fire and screaming. "Hoping like hell you're all done fucking around on your walkabouts pretty damned soon so you can get over here and save our asses."

Baba Yaga's eyes narrowed. "You three okay?"

"We're okay for now," John cut in. "Just don't take *too* long."

Baba Yaga's cackle chilled them to the bone. "Oh, don't worry. I won't."

New Devon, First City, Mercenary Compound Number Two

"Well, *this* all went to shit pretty quickly." Tabitha spat as she hacked the alien weapons.

John and Scott knelt at opposite windows of the turret they'd taken. Their enemies were on all sides, filling the narrow walkways at the top of the wall on each side of the turret and gathered around the base.

John shot one mercenary after another as he considered the options. "We only need to hold out until the others get here."

Tabitha tossed a piece of the machinery out with a clang. "Like I don't fucking *know* that already?"

"It's not like we have gone on a rampage. If we wanted

to, we could just kick it up to eleven." John continued shooting.

Scott hissed softly as a projectile whizzed past his ear. "Where the fuck do they keep *coming* from? It's like every video game ever. This many goons usually means there's something they want to protect." He risked a quick glance out of the window. "Shit, we have *more* incoming."

John looked out at the approaching ships. "How many fucking soldiers *are* there on this planet?" He fired into the seething mass outside the window, the high-velocity flechettes obliterating each mercenary they hit plus the five or six behind the target.

Tabitha's reply was muffled. "Maybe it's the only thing that pays around here."

"Apart from crime, you mean?" Scott leaned back to give his wrists a rest from the pounding they were getting from using his pistols on Level Ten. "How are you managing those on eleven?" he asked John incredulously. "You know that's a joke setting?"

"It's only a joke if you can't handle it. My wife made these with me in mind." John winked and fired again. "I could go to twelve."

Scott surreptitiously dialed his JD Specials up.

The narrow walkways were slick with the blood of many species, and yet still they kept coming, spurred on by the knowledge it was three against their full forces.

"Has the Pod got a flamethrower?" Scott asked. "I know we can't puck the walls without fucking ourselves, but maybe we can burn them off?"

"I do not have a flamethrower," the Pod's EI confirmed.

Tabitha looked up and made a face, scrunching her nose. "Shit. That would have been useful *and* cool."

"Let's see about getting some backup of our own." John opened a link to Bethany Anne. "Hey, boss. How long until you ride in on your white horse?"

Baba Yaga's voice ground out in their ears. "I'm a little busy here. One minute." There was a series of wet thuds in the background. "Son of a scuzz-guzzling scrote-ripping cock-bobbin! That went in my *mouth*, you ass!"

John looked up. Three of the ships had peeled off to surround the turret. "Um, never mind. You just finish up there and then come and give us a hand, yeah?"

Baba Yaga let out a throaty chuckle. "We're done. Gabrielle's team is on their way to you already. They'll be there before us."

"Good, then we'll try our best not to die before you get here."

"Make sure you do," she told him. "You don't have my permission to die on such a lame-ass planet."

He cut the link and looked up. The ships were all aiming at the turret. "Tabitha? Please tell me you have those fucking things working."

"I'm in." Tabitha tapped at her tablet, which had multiple lines running to the big alien guns. They swiveled upward to point at the looming ships, and she pressed the button with a feral grin.

"Say sayonara, motherfuckers."

New Devon, First City, Mercenary Compound Number Two

Gabrielle pounded the arm of her seat. "Can't we go any faster?"

"We cannot," the Pod's EI replied. "However, we will arrive in less than a minute."

"That will have to do," she grumped.

Eric pointed at the sky over the compound. "Fuck, what's going on there? It's raining fire." He opened the link. "We're just outside your location. Where do you need us?"

Tabitha panted over the link, "Holy shit, can you not see the burning ships? We're under all of that."

The Pod swooped in to hover beside one of the burning ships above the turret.

Gabrielle pulled the door open and jumped, pistols drawn. Eric and Darryl were less than a second behind her.

They landed on the right side of the wall and dashed toward the turret, shooting anyone still foolish enough to still be there while the burning ships rained molten metal on the wall.

The door opened and Tabitha's head appeared, followed by her big-ass rifle. "We cool?"

Gabrielle nodded. "We've got you covered on this side."

The cover provided by the burning ships began to peter out, and the mercenaries started to leave the safety of the building again. They made straight for the walls.

Tabitha had her rifle ready. "Do they want to die or something?"

John shrugged and raised his pistols. "Most do."

"Incoming!"

The yell in their ears had them ducking behind the lip of the wall just as two pucks hit the middle of the compound's yard. The mercenaries were knocked flying by the shockwave.

Baba Yaga's Pod came to rest on the mound created by the puck impacts, then the door opened.

Two points of red light shone out of the open door, and they advanced.

She *pushed* fear in heavy waves, incapacitating the mercenaries. To a person they fell to the ground, many sobbing from the abject terror Baba Yaga was instilling in them, from both the fear she was *pushing* and her reputation over the decades of her existence. She was the horror of the human Empress, the Witch in the darkness, the nightmare become *real*.

You're laying it on a bit thick, my love, Michael whispered in her mind.

Hell, yes. Don't spoil my fun.

Baba Yaga eschewed the rough ground altogether. She stepped out of the Pod and walked across the air.

Up on the wall, Tabitha burst out laughing. "Oh, *Jesus*."

No, I'm not, Baba Yaga replied. **I just don't want to get scratches or mud on these boots.**

High Tortuga, Hidden Space Fleet Base, Nursery

The nursery was lit by the Interactive Recreation Training tool, which Phyrro had co-opted to turn the back half of the nursery into a 3-D theatre. The projection painted the corners of the room in shades of blue and gray. The twins huddled on a beanbag and shared a blanket, both utterly transfixed by the heavily-edited version of the events on New Devon.

"Who are those people on the ground?" Alexis asked. "Why are they scared of Mommy?"

"They are bad people, children," Phyrro told them gently. He was programmed to nurture as well as educate. "They work for people who hurt others."

Alexis sniffed and stifled a yawn. "But there's no blood!"

Gabriel nodded. "I know, right?"

They snuggled up, lulled by the rhythm of the unfolding battle.

Alexis pointed at the roof of a building that looked like the front had collapsed. "Look, there's Daddy. He's going to catch those bad guys before they escape!"

Phyrro chuckled. "You two are definitely your parents' children."

Gabriel's eyes were fixed firmly on the screen. "Mommy is making them stop hurting people."

"That was not a question," Phyrro queried.

Gabriel shook his sleepy head without shifting his gaze. "I know."

CHAPTER SEVEN

New Devon, First City, Mercenary Compound Number Two, Shipyard

Baba Yaga crossed the compound and entered the ship-yard, continuing to *push* fear ahead of her. She came down to the ground but used a little buffer of Etheric energy to remain just a touch above it as she walked.

She brought her arms up and willed the Etheric energy to appear. It coated her hands in red light and she *pulled* until more energy than she had dared hold outside of the Dome was concentrated in her upturned palms. She allowed the excess to drip as she passed over the merce-naries on her way to the main building. Her hair rippled behind her, as did her cloak.

I'd like to talk about this look when we get home. Michael's voice was silky in her mind.

Stay on task, she told him sternly.

I'm always on task, he replied. *It's called multi-tasking for a reason. Time-slicing too.*

"I'm in position," he grumped in her ear.

We'll talk about it later, she told him with a small smile. "ArchAngel?"

ArchAngel's reply was instant and eager in her ear. "Yes, Mother? Do you have a task for me?"

Baba Yaga smiled. "Yes. Make sure none of the ships leave the atmosphere. Any that try, terminate them with extreme prejudice."

ArchAngel's voice dropped into a growl. "Yes, Mother."

"Then what the fuck are we waiting for?" Baba Yaga raised her hands and threw the energy at the front of the building. The doors and all the surrounding stonework started melting, running down like a Dali painting. "Why are you all still on the top of that wall?" she called over the comm. "Get your asses over here, or you're gonna miss all the fun."

Baba Yaga advanced one magnificent boot at a time through the melted ruin, cutting through to where the remainder of the mercenaries were scrambling for their ships.

It was too late.

She jumped onto a platform and released bolts of super-concentrated Etheric energy into the rising ships, willing them to act like Jean's flechettes—the explosive ones.

The results were pretty much what she had expected.

Ships dropped out of the sky as Baba Yaga hit them with bolt after bolt of red, blue, and white energy. The mercenaries poured from their ships, angry now that Baba Yaga had dropped the fear and they could think straight again.

She was joined by Michael, who approached with fire in his eyes and Etheric energy moving over his arms. *I can't tell you how much I'm enjoying this opportunity to cut loose.* He punctuated his greeting with a knife-hand strike that cut the attacking soldier in two.

Baba Yaga wrinkled her nose at the smell. **Maybe I'll ramp up the fear just a touch less next time.** She pulled again on the Etheric. **Here, honey.** She filled the air around Michael with enough power to fry a human being.

He had a moment of confusion as the energy hit him. *Is it my birthday?*

She snickered. *No.*

I have not forgotten an anniversary of some sort?

Baba Yaga's dark chuckle cut the night, giving the advancing hordes pause. Her inner voice was all Bethany Anne. **No, dear. Can't a wife just spoil her husband every now and then? Just feel for the energy. You should be able to keep pulling it once you start. Just don't go too far.**

The air around Michael began to crackle as he shaped the energy to his will. *I love that you knew I needed this.* He looked at his wife, who was wearing what he secretly termed her "hotness from hell" face.

She shrugged barely imperceptibly in the almost-darkness. **You deserve a release. I have been riding you pretty hard about the dinosaur thing.**

She held a finger up, and then with a wave of the same hand flung the ball of Etheric energy she made appear into some nearby mercenaries. **However, that is not an endorsement. I'm not budging on it.**

I didn't think you would. Forked lightning streaked from Michael's hands to the sky, causing three more ships to explode in midair. One of the ships took out two others on its descent.

Baba Yaga had an idea. *I saw something interesting last time I was in the Dome...*

Oh yes?

Can you throw sheet lightning?

I can certainly try. What do you have in mind?

She volleyed energy balls at a pair of ships that were trying to use the wreckage of the others to evade destruction. *We need to clear some space to work*, she told him as the ships crashed to the ground.

Michael's eyes alighted on a group of mercenaries who were using a downed ship as cover to take potshots at them. Ineffective, but annoying. *Not for long.*

Tabitha strutted into the shipyard.

Every second step she took, she fired and a mercenary dropped. "Will you two get a fucking room already? It's been bad enough with the love-fest back at the base." A loud shot followed the snarky comment from behind them, turning a nearby Leath's head into a fine spray. She patted the rifle fondly. "I knew Gracie here was worth the effort of pounding the shit out of that Shrillexian."

John and Eric appeared a moment later, followed by Gabrielle. Scott and Darryl brought up the rear. They moved as one across the shipyard, taking out clusters of mercenaries as they worked their way to the platform.

"Good of you to join us," Baba Yaga snarked aloud. "Now if it's not too much trouble, do you think you can all keep these assholes off us while we have a little fun grounding those ships?"

They got to work clearing the ground, and Baba Yaga and Michael turned their eyes to the skies.

New Devon, Above Mercenary Compound Number Two, Lead Ship *The Reaver*

The company commander swiveled his chair from one side of the bridge to the other, mouth agape. Electricity rent the air below the ship, and the commander stared in disbelief as his fleet and the ships of his allies were destroyed in rippling volleys of light. "What the holy hell is happening down there?"

None of the stations answered.

"Somebody fucking tell me *something!*" he roared. "Who are these assholes? Why aren't we dropping kinetics on them?"

A youngish Noel-ni turned in his chair. "I can tell you, but you won't believe me."

The commander was apoplectic by this point. "*Well?*"

The Noel-ni nodded. "They are humans, sir. There appear to be eight of them."

"*Eight?* You're telling me that just eight humans did all *this?*" The commander swept a hand toward the viewscreen, where the partially liquefied remains of his life's achievement sat at a strange angle to the ground.

The Noel-ni shook his head. "I'm telling you that *one* of the humans did that."

"One?" the commander whispered. "Who are these humans?"

"I have footage if you want to see it, sir."

The commander nodded blankly.

The viewscreen changed from the bird's eye view of the ruined compound to a vid of it in its earlier condition from a lower angle. Two kinetics hit the compound, and the tiny ship landed. The door opened and the soldiers fell to the ground, and then the human emerged.

"Freeze it there," the commander told Communications. He couldn't make out the features with the resolution, only the red eyes set in inky-black skin. "Zoom in on the face."

The communications officer turned in her seat. "Commander, we're being contacted."

The commander snarled. "Ignore it! Ready the kinetics, and show me that face!"

"Umm, sir?"

Every soul on the bridge stared at the screen when it suddenly filled with red eyes and far too many teeth.

The commander howled with rage and began to gesticulate wildly at the screen. "You...you..."

"Me, *what*?" the face asked.

"You are the human below," he finished lamely.

ArchAngel snickered, which looked terrifying on Baba Yaga's face. "Okay, we'll go with that."

The commander pushed away the chill that laugh caused to run down his spine. "You will all die for what you've done," he told the human on the screen. "You can't just come here and—"

The human interrupted with a growl and a flash of its red eyes. "Oh great, we have a *monologuer*. How fucking boring. Save it, asshole. I have no time to waste on scum like you. I have a job to do."

The commander, unused to being spoken to with

anything less than deference, drew himself up and gestured to the tech to return his feed to the ground below. She looked at him and shook her head. He turned to weapons and got the nod that the kinetics were ready to be released.

The human's face shifted. "It's almost sweet. You think you have a chance."

Was that... Was it *laughing* at him? The commander matched the human's smug expression with a smarmy grin of his own. "You are hardly in a position to mock since we are up here with all the weaponry and you are down there with no way of defending against it."

"That's just priceless! Funny, I was about to say the same thing." The human let out a cold laugh, and *The Reaver* shuddered.

The commander started as the bridge was inundated with alarms and warning lights. "What the fuck was *that?*"

All amusement faded from the human's face in an instant. "If you had paid more attention to where you were going instead of where you'd been, let's just say you might have avoided this outcome."

The human was suddenly gone, and the screen returned to showing the outside of the ship. The clouds ahead disgorged a massive ship, its deadly lines cutting the air as it drew closer.

The face of death replaced the wave of projectiles on the screen. "Then again, my Queen *did* order extreme prejudice. Sucks to be a scumbag today. Later, *assholes!*"

The human vanished, and the commander came to his senses just as the kinetics hit his ship. *The Reaver* bucked and twisted under the continued barrage, and he fell to his knees as his ship screamed its death throes. It was too late for him.

For the whole crew.

The klaxons wailed, cutting off any chance of a final coherent thought before his ship disintegrated.

The *ArchAngel II* sliced through the falling debris toward the surface. As she came in to hover above the burning conflagration below, she heard her mother curse.

"Fucksticks! How did one get away?"

CHAPTER EIGHT

New Devon, First City, Mercenary Compound Number Two

Baba Yaga stood with one boot on the large mercenary's chest. She leaned over to ensure that the Shrillexian heard her clearly. "I don't care what the fuck planet you came from. I don't even care how things *used* to work around here. This is how they work *now*."

Baba Yaga read the crowd's agitation. This was way beyond anything they'd ever experienced. Most were just ordinary citizens, and they were afraid and angry. They gathered in front of the compound and the human who had just bitch-slapped a full-sized Shrillexian into submission.

"You can't just come here and start telling us how to live! This was why we left the fucking Empire in the first place—to get away from the likes of you."

Baba Yaga gave the speaker credit for bravery. However, she wasn't going to let *him* know that.

She turned her impassive gaze on him, tilting her head slightly. "That is *exactly* what I am doing, so spread the word." She raised her voice so all could hear. "It's my way or the highway, so shut the fuck up or ship out of here, because the old ways are *done*. Your decision to live like it's the Wild-fucking-West has cost the *last* innocent person their life." She swept an accusing hand over the crowd. "You are all to blame, so listen up. I am the Mistress of this planet now, and I will run it as I see fit. As it is, I see no issue with most of it. If you all want to spend your lives fucking, fighting, and getting high instead of building something you can be proud of, it's your life to waste. However, there will be no slave trade on New Devon, and the fights will be fair."

Whispers went through the crowd.

"*New* Devon?"

"There's already a Devon. It's a worse shithole than this place."

"Whatever. It's a no-go zone now." The Zhyn who'd spoken looked at Baba Yaga, then at the kind of familiar looking humans in her guard. Recognition hit, and the Zhyn began to edge backward.

The Witch held up a hand containing a ball of energy that was still bright even against the encroaching dawn. "It is perfectly obvious that you cannot rule yourselves."

A protest rippled through the crowd at that.

Baba Yaga raised the hand. "ENOUGH! You allowed the slavers to take control. Your illusion of freedom was just that—a *fantasy*. My rule will not be complicated since on my planets there is only *one* rule." She *pushed* fear and sent the ball of energy into the air to dissipate and rain down on the crowd as she spoke.

"Do not piss me off."

Above New Devon, QBS *ArchAngel II*, Bethany Anne's Quarters

Bethany Anne looked down at the gore encrusting her from head-to-thigh. Her boots, however, were still clean. She smiled at them fondly as she pulled them off one at a time, then made a face when she caught sight of herself in the mirror. "I need a shower."

She opened the door to her bathroom just as Michael emerged wearing clean, loose clothing.

He grinned disarmingly as he dried his hair with one of her soft towels. "I am wondering why your bathroom is much better equipped than mine?"

Bethany Anne left a bloody kiss-print on his cheek as she slipped past him. "Queen's privileges, my love. I'll see you in the meeting room when I'm done."

As the hot water pounded the battle aches away, she considered exactly how much effort she wanted to put into managing a whole other planet. The answer was, not much at all.

She would put in some structure—basic laws, for one— but otherwise, she would honor her word and allow things to run mostly as they had before. Besides, the vibe here was just right for the rebels she'd promised to take care of.

New Devon was wild, but now she'd cleaned out the worst of the rat nests it was the *right* kind of wild.

Bethany Anne tapped the table with her fingers. "Okay, so we've cleaned up the pirate playground."

"Mercenary," John corrected.

She arched an eyebrow. "Close enough. Now, what's next for this place? How do we get it running to meet our needs without interfering too much with the basic structure of the society here?" She looked around the table. "Tabitha."

Tabitha looked around in surprise. "Why're you asking me? I enforced the law for a hell of a lot longer than I spent breaking it." She sniffed and went back to picking through the fruit bowl on the table. "But I suppose it wouldn't be too much of a stretch to put a little regulation on those fights."

Bethany Anne resumed tapping her fingers on the table. "If they're regulated, and we turn prizefighting into a desirable career, there would be less reason to join the mercenaries." She looked at Michael. "Do I remember you talking about something like that?"

He nodded. "This is exactly why I wanted to establish some kind of entertainment industry on High Tortuga. If the people are focused on feeling good, they're not focused on the minor gripes that cumulatively lead to dissent."

"True," Gabrielle agreed. "It would be a good thing to have a Guardian Marine presence on-world, though. I know we haven't seen the last of the slave traders."

Bethany Anne frowned. "Yeah, I don't like that a few of them got away."

John grunted unconcernedly. "It doesn't matter. We'll track them down."

Tabitha folded her arms. "Well, whoever comes here next will take care of them." She nodded toward Bethany Anne and Gabrielle. "We've got a shopping date."

High Tortuga, Space Fleet Base, Hangar Bay

The hangar was a hive of activity as the first rotation of Guardian Marines prepared to deploy to New Devon.

Bethany Anne pointed out one of the shuttle bays, where Sabine, Jacqueline, Mark, and Ricole waited near the shuttle with barely concealed impatience to be on their way.

"Come *on*, already!" Sabine's voice carried across the hangar.

Ricole paced in front of the Pod.

Michael turned to Bethany Anne. "Excuse me for a moment."

Bethany Anne nodded, already sidetracked by a bunch of people needing her attention. She held a finger up, then pointed at Michael. "You have until he's done, then we're going to see our children."

Sabine turned at Michael's touch on her shoulder. "You four are going to New Devon?"

Mark was reasonably cool, but Jacqueline's energy was almost tangible in its intensity. Ricole's eyes roamed the hangar, watching the shuttles leave with longing.

Sabine grinned, her eyes dark with anticipation. "Where else? It is actually the five of us. We are just waiting on Demon."

Demon is here. The enhanced mountain lion padded into sight, eighty kilos of solid tawny muscle. The crowd parted before her as she sauntered toward them, tail flicking slowly from side to side. She sat down beside Michael and tilted her chin imperiously. *Let the hunt commence.*

Sabine and the others grabbed their gear and began to load the shuttle while Demon affected boredom.

Michael smiled to himself. He enjoyed the cat's dry snark immensely. She'd come a long way from the twitchy wreck she'd been when he'd rescued her from a lab back on Earth. "How are you, Demon? Have you had any good hunting lately?"

Demon lifted a velvet paw and flicked out four needle-sharp claws. *Plenty. This planet is full of creatures that don't know well enough to fear me. I have been more than able to feed myself here.*

Michael raised an eyebrow. "Then why go to New Devon?"

Demon languidly stood when Sabine waved her over. *Because I want to fight.*

High Tortuga, Space Fleet Base, Queen's Suite

Jean was reading on the couch when they returned.

Bethany Anne had left John and Michael behind and breezed straight through to the nursery to see the children without even stopping to greet Jean. She paused at the door when she saw them curled up fast asleep together on the beanbag.

Michael peered at them over her shoulder when he caught up. "Seems a shame to wake them."

Bethany Anne looked at the freeze-frame of Baba Yaga at the back of the room and her brow knitted. "I think they can sleep a few minutes more. I need to have a word with Jean." She turned and marched back to the living area.

Michael glanced at the screen, then at the children. He shrugged and pulled the door closed in case the children were awakened by their mother tearing their aunt a new one for whatever it was Bethany Anne thought Jean had done.

When he returned to the living area, Bethany Anne was standing in front of Jean with her hands on her hips. John stood behind Bethany Anne, shaking his head to tell her to take it seriously. He looked from one to the other. "What is the issue?"

Bethany Anne pointed at Jean, her voice a low hiss. "She showed our children footage of the fight!"

Jean shook her head. "It wasn't raw footage."

Bethany Anne glared. "So you aren't the only one I should be pissed at. Phyrro, how could you let this happen?"

The EI's avatar appeared on the wallscreen. "I was rather skeptical about allowing the children access to the footage, but Jean made a good argument for me permitting them to watch. I *did* edit the footage." Phyrro played the nursery-cam footage of the twins' reactions. "I believe they learned something important from the experience."

Bethany Anne narrowed her eyes at the screen. "You're not getting away with it that easily," she told Jean.

"What, like you did?" Jean grinned. "Seriously, lighten up! I wouldn't have let them see anything they shouldn't.

They learned where they come from tonight, BA. They were damn proud of you both."

Bethany Anne pursed her lips, not entirely convinced. "We're not done talking about this." She turned to Michael. "Let's get the children back into their beds."

They made their way back to the nursery. Alexis stirred as Bethany Anne gently worked her arms underneath the girl to lift her. Her daughter wrapped her arms around her mother instinctively as she picked her up.

Michael picked Gabriel up, and they took the children to their beds. Bethany Anne ducked to enter Alexis' Pod-crib.

The motion was enough to wake her for a brief moment. "Mommy, are you and Daddy home from your date now?"

Bethany Anne gazed into her daughter's eyes, unable, as she always was when she looked at her children, to believe that she and Michael had created such wonder. "Yes, sweetie. Daddy and I are home. I believe you saw some of what Daddy and I did tonight. Were you or Gabriel scared?"

Alexis laughed and clung tighter to Bethany Anne, nuzzling into her neck. "No, Mommy. But you're much prettier *without* your makeup on." She yawned and her eyelashes fluttered closed. "I love you, Mommy."

"Love you more." Bethany Anne kissed her forehead. "Goodnight, my angel."

Gabriel hadn't woken up when Michael moved him. She ducked into his Pod-crib and kissed him, too, and she and Michael left the nursery.

"Will you give Jean a break now?" Michael asked.

"Yeah," Jean called from the living area. "Will you give me a break?"

Bethany Anne made a face. "I suppose I may have been a little loose and free with your kids." She shrugged a little uncomfortably at the realization.

"And everyone else's," John supplied.

Bethany Anne put a hand to her forehead and sighed. "Go on, rub it in."

Jean came over and patted her shoulder. "Don't sweat it. You were a good aunt, and you did all the kids good. It's just so sweet to finally be able to return the favor."

Bethany Anne sensed Michael's amusement. She turned and caught the smirk he didn't hide quickly enough.

"What?" he asked, looking around. "Do I still have a spot of blood on my face?"

CHAPTER NINE

High Tortuga, Space Fleet Base, Security Pit, Meeting Area

"We are almost ready to complete the seclusion of High Tortuga. Or, as I'm code-naming it, 'Project Boxing Ring.'" Bethany Anne put her tablet on the table and took a sip of her Coke. "The Guardian Marine teams are arriving on New Devon as we speak. They will instill some order in the first and second cities—however it is they need to do that—and continue the emancipation of the miners out by the lakes."

Peter chuckled. "There was some competition to get on *that* assignment."

Bethany Anne smirked. "I'll just bet. That place is the answer to many problems, not least creating another layer in the frontier for the interdiction I want."

"How do you mean?" Gabrielle asked. "I know we like it as a place for the rabble-rousers, but how will that help us keep undesirables from finding High Tortuga?"

"I didn't need to take over a whole planet to find a place where people could blow off some steam." She leaned forward and laced her hands together on the table. "New Devon is going to be the place people end up if they try to find *old* Devon. Then, depending on their intent, we can either divert them or transport them here."

Tabitha tapped the table. "Or, you know, fuck them up completely if they're there to start something."

Bethany Anne snickered. "That, too. So now we have the shuttle service in place—thank you for getting those Gate engines for the bus-ship built so quickly, William— we can get our rebels taken care of."

William nodded. "Wasn't anything. It went faster once Eve finished Michael's project and had some time for it."

Bethany Anne raised an eyebrow at her husband.

"Nothing you need to let bother you," Michael assured her. "Just a little something we came up with to help with Alexis and Gabriel's education."

She gave Michael a look. *You can tell me about it later. Now isn't the time.*

"So how do we divert the whole galaxy to the wrong planet?" Jean asked. "I mean, we can't exactly change the maps."

"Yes, we can," ADAM replied through the speaker. "I'm ready to implement the virus for Project Reroute that will replace the coordinates of High Tortuga with those of New Devon."

The Queen rolled her eyes. "Let's just codename it 'Devon.'"

Tabitha leaned back in her chair. "Yeah, because yet

another name in the 'what the fuck planet are we on' game was *just* what we needed."

Bethany Anne waved her off impatiently and turned to look at William expectantly. "What about getting some normality around here? Now we have the planet's infrastructure under control, I want to loosen travel restrictions." She narrowed her eyes at the reactions around the table. "Once we're in Phase Three, that is. Nobody is getting on or off High Tortuga without my say-so until I can be sure they have no way of running their mouths about our location to the highest bidder."

William shrugged. "I don't know what you want me to say. Until we figure out how to loosen travel restrictions without High Tortuga's location becoming common knowledge, Phase Three can't go ahead."

"You know how I feel about the word 'can't.' It just doesn't sit well with me." She wrinkled her nose. "We're almost there with this."

Michael was grateful for the centuries of practice he'd had keeping his face straight. "There is still the practical issue of removing the information from large numbers of people."

Akio nodded, resting his chin on his hand. "There is also the moral issue to consider. What if we take more than High Tortuga's location?"

"We can't risk that." Bethany Anne made a face. "Keep on it, and get with anyone you need to find the solution. Next item, my absence."

Tabitha grinned. *"Finally."*

"I have to agree." Gabrielle pushed her hair back from

her eyes. "I'm more than a little excited for some family time and retail therapy."

"Therapy?" Bethany Anne shook her head. "It's not going to be therapy for the store owners. Mama needs some new pumps."

Jean snorted. "Does Mama *need* some new pumps, or does Mama just *want* some new pumps?"

Bethany Anne pointed at Jean. "You're still on my shit list. Be glad I'm even taking you with me."

Jean winked. "Quite happy to stay behind. It'll save me another fight with Lillian. You'll just have to find someone else who can fly the ship."

Bethany Anne rolled her eyes.

"I don't know why you're so mad," Gabrielle pointed out. "It wasn't like she showed the twins a certain movie that we can't talk about because it would be breaking the rules."

John let out a burst of laughter. "Shit, she's got you there, BA! That was too fucking funny."

"Yes," Gabrielle snarked. "It was just the *funniest* when Eric and I were called into the Academy to explain why our twelve-year-olds and their friends suddenly started showing up at school with bruises they refused to explain."

Bethany Anne held a finger up and opened her mouth to argue, then dropped it, closed her mouth, and shook her head. Her shoulders slumped. "Nope, I've got nothing to say in my own defense."

The chuckles started.

New Devon, First City, Main Shipyard

Jacqueline inhaled as she stepped off the shuttle ramp behind Mark. "This place smells like..." She sniffed again, her nose wrinkling.

Death, Demon finished for her. The cat padded down the ramp and came to stand beside Jacqueline and Mark.

Sabine swaggered past with her bags, chuckling. "I heard they had a recent outbreak of it." She turned back, one hand on her hip. "Well, are you just going to stand around staring all day, or are we going to find a place to stay?"

They exited the shuttle bay and made their way over to the line for the orientation desk, where they were given directions to temporary accommodation and a link to their ops handler for the duration of their stay.

The orientation officer winked as she passed Sabine the information. "Get settled in first, and enjoy a night in the city before you check in with ops."

Mark grinned and nodded at a string of bars along the main strip. "We won't lack for nightlife here."

Ricole swept the streets with her gaze, ever alert to the prospect of danger. "We'll need jobs to pay for all that." She noted that they were drawing attention. An older Noel-ni looked from Ricole to the humans and nodded at her. "What's that all about?" she asked aloud.

The corner of Sabine's mouth lifted up a fraction. "They know you're a badass, in the company of the baddest of badasses."

Ricole glanced at the watchers as they walked. Was this respect? She wasn't certain, but she was sure that not all the watchers had pure intentions. She shrugged and followed the others.

After dropping their gear at the hotel, they returned to the main strip and walked toward the bazaar until they came to a likely-looking bar.

Sabine pointed out a sign above the door that translated to You Break It, You Pay. (Unless it's your face on someone's fist. That's on you).

Jacqueline grinned and pushed open the door. "My kind of place."

Mark rolled his eyes.

They were seated with glasses of something darkly golden and the discussion about their options was well underway when the doors opened and spilled a crowd of already intoxicated assholes into the bar.

The mixed group of Torcellans, Queegert, two T'lorns and a Zhyn caused a scene as they crossed to the bar, where they clamored until the bartender served them.

Jacqueline was far from impressed by the interruption to what had been a pleasant evening so far. "Holy shit, is there no bar in the galaxy where you can just enjoy a quiet drink without a bunch of douchenozzles like these crashing it?"

Sabine's lip curled as she looked them over. "Apparently not," she murmured. "But then, that was true on Earth as well."

The rowdy drunks roared as one as one of them made a comment in their own language about humans being comparable to a sexually transmitted disease in that they spread without mercy and had no known cure.

The four understood perfectly, thanks to the translation implants in their heads. Jacqueline made to get up when another mocked Ricole, calling her a pet.

Mark touched her arm to hold her back. "Not worth it, babe."

The waitress, who was exchanging their empty glasses for full ones, took one look at the assholes propping up the bar and turned to Jacqueline with sympathy on her face. "Ignore them. They just don't like being knocked off the top of the pole. Most were glad of the Mistress' intervention on behalf of the slaves after we realized she wasn't going to mess with our lives. Those who aren't? Well, they'll come around, or they won't."

"If they don't, we will have something to do while we're here." Sabine smirked and put her empty glass on the waitress' tray. "What is life like here?"

The waitress gave Sabine a wide smile. "It's a hard planet. There are fights and the occasional murder, but otherwise...you know." She shrugged. "Same as any place on the edge, I suspect. We do what needs doing to get on. Folks around here don't handle authority too well."

Mark chuckled at that. He was keeping one eye on Jacqueline, who was still listening in on the shambles at the bar. They were getting louder and more daring since they thought the four couldn't understand them.

"You see how weak he is. We could take the females from him with no problem."

"I want that one." The Torcellan screamed in pain as the bones in the hand he was pointing in Jacqueline's direction were crushed to splinters inside the skin.

Ricole did a double-take, looking at Mark's empty chair and then at the bar, where Mark had forced the speaker to his knees with a little pressure in the right place on the broken hand. "You owe the lady an apology," he growled into the mercenary's face. "Disrespect me all you like, but you keep your fucking mouth shut about my woman."

He headbutted the whimpering douchebag and stood to face the rest of them, who had all moved to surround him.

Jacqueline's eyes shone yellow. She affected a huge sigh and looked at Sabine and Ricole with a sly grin. "Well, I suppose I'd better give my boy toy a hand."

"Claws might come in handy," Ricole supplied.

Sabine snickered. "Go, have fun," she told Jacqueline. "Ricole and I will ensure the fight stays fair." She patted the pistols on her hips.

Jacqueline grinned, and in the next instant grew much taller, hairier, and deadlier. She threw herself into the melee with flash of claws and fangs. "I'm cooominnng forrr youuu!"

Sabine got Ricole's attention, then nodded to the pair. "I thought we'd be here at least a day before she went all Pricolici on someone's ass," she commented dryly. She stood and stretched nonchalantly. "Where shall we work from?"

Ricole pointed at the bar. "Seems as good a place as any."

They made their way over chairs, under two tables, and ducked a body, then vaulted up onto the bar, pistols drawn. The bar was in an uproar as the fight spread through the patrons. Sabine threw her head back and shrieked her joy at being in the midst of it all again.

She and Ricole kept watch from their perch.

A few of the people surrounding Jacqueline and Mark drew their weapons. "Yeah, no. Not happening," Sabine yelled, startling the mob into looking at her. She waved her pistol over the crowd. "Two of them versus as many of you as are stupid enough to take them on. That's fair enough." She indicated that they should carry on, and more than a few looked at Sabine, wondering about her crazy logic and if she'd completely lost it. "I meant it," she assured them with a sparkling smile. "This should be fun to watch."

Ricole glared at them all like she'd just stepped in them on the street. "You heard the woman. *Fight!*" She picked up a glass and threw it at one of the original assholes.

It was enough to break the tension. As if a switch had been thrown, the bar erupted into a chaos of swinging stools and smashing glasses.

One of the bartenders looked up at the young Noel-ni and shook his head.

Orian looked up as Keet shoved his hairy head through the door. "There's a big fight down the street. Some humans are taking on all comers."

Orian jumped to his feet, as did a few others. They'd all talked about picking a fight with one of the humans, but an opportunity to back it up with action was not to be missed.

At least, that was their plan.

The street outside was packed with onlookers. They watched the events inside the bar through the large windows, open-mouthed. Orian followed Keet through the crowd to the bar, and they pushed inside.

From the threshold, they took in the circle of unconscious bodies around the human...and a large canine of some kind? Those two plowed through the rush of oncoming attackers, and they both appeared to be having a huge amount of fun doing it.

Orian exchanged a glance with Keet, and they looked back at the ruckus. When they drew their weapons, they were met by the cold stares and long barrels of the human and the Noel-ni on the bar.

"No guns!" the human female yelled at them.

The Noel-ni flashed her canines as an unconscious form hit the wall behind the bar and slid down. Her smile didn't make the two feel any better.

"Feel free to try and hit them, though," she told them.

CHAPTER TEN

High Tortuga, Space Fleet Base, Queen's Suite, Nursery

Bethany Anne pressed the lid of the suitcase down. It took some of her considerable strength, but she finally managed to pull the zipper most of the way closed. "Balls!" She stuck the finger she'd pinched in her mouth to relieve the sting.

Michael appeared in the doorway, coffee mug in hand. "Need a hand?"

She shook her head and finished zipping the bag. "I've got it."

Michael smirked. "I believe you owe a forfeit for that little outburst. Now, what rare and exquisite penalty does one choose when it's entirely likely you will not slip again?"

Bethany Anne shook the sore finger at her husband. "I didn't slip *this* time. Could have been talking about any balls at all. It's not my problem if you have a fixation."

"Hmmm." Michael looked a little too disappointed.

"You'll have to get up a lot earlier in the day if you want to catch me out, honey." She smirked, took the mug from his hand, and drained it. She grimaced slightly at the after-taste. "It's not quite coffee, but it's not completely horrible either."

Michael retrieved the mug and took it to the kitchen to get a refill. He called back, "You could pick up some of that Yollin blend I like while you're away!"

"Shouldn't be a problem. We're taking an extra storage cube with us. If there's anything else you want while we're there, get a list together."

He returned with his refill and a cold Coke for Bethany Anne. "How are you feeling about returning to the *Meredith Reynolds*?"

She took the bottle and sat down beside him on the couch. "Excited. It's been too long since I've seen baby Kevin."

Michael smiled. "He is not a baby any longer."

"I know. Apparently, he's a complete terror." She put her feet up on the ottoman and chuckled. "Although I'm pretty sure Dad and Patricia are having an easier parenting experience than we are." She wrinkled her nose as her concerns surfaced. "Mostly excited."

Michael gave her a knowing look. "Your father's problem?"

"Yeah. I'm not going to butt in…" Michael gave her a look that said he knew better. "Unless he asks," she conceded. "What have you got planned for the children while I'm away?" She looked sideways at her husband. "You were acting cagey earlier."

Michael's mouth twitched. "I have a couple of field trips planned for them. Nothing too big."

"'Nothing too big?'" Bethany Anne narrowed her eyes, not buying his innocent expression for one second. "No dinosaur hunting with the children, Michael."

Michael held a hand up. "Of course not. What I have planned is strictly educational."

Bethany Anne's tone was clear. "Alexis and Gabriel will not leave the safety of the base while I'm away."

They heard the children approaching, so Michael quickly explained into Bethany Anne's mind.

When he finished, Bethany Anne was completely nonplussed. *Huh? You just told me you were planning field trips.*

Michael winked. *That's what I want the children to think. Eve has completed a project I had her working on. The challenge has been keeping it from our daughter.*

She stood as the children burst into the living area with all of their usual enthusiasm, and a little extra for their mother. *I suppose that's okay. Just remember, I will be coming home. It will not be pleasant to be you if I find out you took our babies out to hunt that damned dinosaur of yours.*

She took a knee and pulled Alexis and Gabriel close, inhaling deeply to fix their scents in her mind. It was hard to leave them again so soon. "I wish I could take you both with me." She kissed them all over their faces. "My delicious ones."

"Yuck, Mommy," Gabriel protested, squirming in her arms and swiping his arm across his face. "You don't have to make a big deal out of it. You're only going for a few days."

She blew a soft raspberry on his cheek and released him. Alexis scooted into the space Gabriel had vacated and wrapped her arms around Bethany Anne's neck. She laid her cheek against her mother's. "Don't worry, Mommy. Daddy will take care of us while you're with Grampy."

Bethany Anne looked at Michael as she stroked her daughter's hair. "That's what I'm worried about, sweetie."

Alexis giggled. "Daddy's not going to lose us."

Bethany Anne laughed. "I guess not." She picked up her luggage in one hand and pointed at Michael. "Remember, no dinosaur hunting." She blew them all one last kiss and was gone.

Alexis ran straight to Michael and turned her shining face up to him. "Are we going *dinosaur* hunting, Daddy?"

Michael smiled enigmatically. "That species' name actually translates as 'Moving Mountain.' Nothing to do with dinosaurs, really."

Alexis gave him a hard look. "That's a technicality."

He nodded. "Yes, my sweet girl. Yes, it is."

Gabriel huffed. "So are we hunting the big lizards or not?"

"No," Michael told him.

Alexis made a sound halfway between disappointment and indignation. "Why did you answer Gabriel so simply? You could have just told me instead of making me sift through your substitution... No, that's not right." She looked up at him. "Your subtext."

"Subtext?" Gabriel frowned. "All he did was tell you the name of the alien dinosaur."

Alexis shrugged. "Word positioning is important."

Michael smiled to himself at the proof his assessment had been right.

"Because your brother does not require the teaching of nuance just yet. He would take the subtlety and run with it."

"Like you are?"

Michael chuckled. "You are your mother's daughter, Alexis. Gabriel has different strengths."

Gabriel frowned. "Huh?"

"It would go over your head right now, son."

Gabriel folded his arms and stuck his chin out. "So what? Just because she's taller than me, it doesn't mean I can't jump high enough and catch it."

Michael ruffled his son's hair. "I know you could, son." His eyes glinted when he considered his plans for his children.

If Bethany Anne would have seen him, she might have thought he was about to cheat somehow.

Devon, First City, Main Strip, Bar

Sabine whooped and kicked a bowl of something vaguely peanut-looking into the Krenlock's eyes before it could grab her legs. She followed through with a swift kick to the face and turned her attention to the door as it opened and another group of wannabes came in looking for trouble.

"Hey, Ricole, we have fresh meat," she called.

The Noel-ni flashed a sharp grin at the newcomers.

"Leave your weapons at the door, and you're welcome to join in."

The group of seven protested. One raised his weapon but jumped back when it flew from his hand. He looked up at the bar, where Sabine kissed the barrel of her Jean Dukes Special and winked at them. "Weapons at the door, boys. Otherwise, you stand and watch while everyone else has fun."

Five of the seven stripped their weapons off and handed them to the two who chose to remain as spectators.

"Fine choice, gentlemen," Sabine called to the two. "If fighting's not your game, how about a little bet?"

Above High Tortuga, Repurposed Leath Ship

Bethany Anne looked around the stateroom and wrinkled her nose. "It's not exactly G'laxix-Sphaea-class comfort."

Jean dumped her bags and turned to Bethany Anne. "It's close enough, right?"

Tabitha went over to look in the fridge. "You have to admit that Leath tech is some of the best, besides the Empire's."

Jean grinned. "That was why I made sure to have this baby stuffed with all the goodies." She flopped down on one of the couches and put her feet up with a long sigh. "This is the most well-earned vacation I've ever taken."

Gabrielle came in at the tail end of Jean's statement. She pushed Jean's feet aside and sat next to her. "You've taken a vacation before? Funny, I didn't think you even knew what the word meant."

Jean scowled and put her feet back up. "I've taken vacations."

Tabitha came back from the fridge loaded down with a little of everything. She sat on the couch opposite and pointed the piece of fruit in her hand at Jean. "It doesn't count as a vacation if you take your work with you." She bit into the fruit. "Take a leaf out of my book. The only thing I'm going to break on this trip is the bank."

Bethany Anne grinned. "You and me both. I can't wait to see what's changed on the *Meredith* since we were last there. A bit more than four years is a long time."

"Ooh, new boutiques," Gabrielle cooed. "I know for a fact there's a new shoe designer you're going to just love." She leaned over and whispered, "Meredith told me about them."

"Maybe…" She held up one foot and examined the wrought metal heel of her pump. "I'm definitely looking forward to expanding my footwear selection."

"Don't forget all our old favorite haunts as well," Tabitha reminded them. "You know I sent my orders ahead as soon as I found out we were heading home. My ass deserves custom leather and fine dining."

Bethany Anne raised an eyebrow. "Don't get noticed."

Jean turned to Bethany Anne and rolled her eyes. "You know, it's a good thing we brought that extra storage cube after all," she admitted. "Glad you made me see sense."

"Don't try to pull that with me. I know for a fact that at least a third of that cube will be taken up with tech when we leave."

Jean laughed and held her hands up. "I'll plead guilty in advance."

Tabitha's shoulders shook with amusement. "So where are we headed first?"

"Family time first," Bethany Anne confirmed. "Then we go shopping."

She grinned. "And then we *dance*."

CHAPTER ELEVEN

High Tortuga, Space Fleet Base

John was standing on the other side of the door when Michael answered it. "You're early."

John grinned. "Couldn't wait to see how Daddy Vampire was coping without any women around to hold his hand." He peeked inside. "Huh, you don't have them stuck to a wall.'"

Michael resisted closing the door on John. He stepped back to let him enter the residence instead. "Daddy Vampire is managing just fine, thank you." He gave John a pointed look. "May I remind you of the first time you were left alone to care for Lillian?"

The children arrived, saving John from further embarrassment.

Alexis let out a happy little squeal when she saw that her favorite uncle had arrived. "Are you coming on the adventure with us?" She waved an imperious finger at him when he nodded that he was.

John looked aside at Michael as he knelt obediently for Alexis to scramble onto his shoulders. "I thought BA nixed your field trip plans?"

Michael shook his head. "I had something planned for that eventuality." He turned to the twins. "Have you got everything?" Satisfied that they did, he swept them toward the door.

Alexis was as curious as ever. "Where *are* we going, Daddy?"

"That's what I want to know," John agreed.

Gabriel held Michael's hand and looked up at his father with trust. "Whatever we do, it will be fun because Mommy's not here to say Dad's going too far."

John snorted behind them. "From the mouths of babes."

Scott and Darryl joined them as they made their way to Michael's office. Eric was waiting outside when they got there.

"Is there anybody else who wants to join us?" Michael asked dryly.

"Just us guys," Scott answered. "Sabine probably would, but she's off-planet. I think she wants to know if you have it in you. Oh, and Jacqueline would as well, and I suppose…"

Michael held up a hand. "That's enough."

Eric shrugged. "We all had to see how this was going to work, I guess."

Michael led them inside, taking the turn to the wing that was still under construction as far as anyone else knew. He ducked through the plastic sheeting into the corridor beyond. "This way," he told them, disappearing through one of the doors.

The room beyond contained a small seating area and four devices that looked like Pod-docs. The entire back wall was given over to a screen, and there was a console beneath it.

Alexis bounced around on John's shoulders until he put her down and ran over to investigate. "They look more like Pod-docs than the IRT-Pods in the nursery." She turned around and tried to raise one eyebrow, but both went up. "What do they do?"

Michael nodded. "These are something a little better than the interactive recreation training tool. This is the next-level IRT, the Vid-doc. It's an immersive experience instead of merely being interactive."

Gabriel's face lit up. "VR?"

Alexis was less than impressed. "Oh, it's just a game. That's *so* Earth tech, Daddy."

Michael opened the lid of the Vid-doc and swept a hand over the inside. "Are you sure about that?"

Alexis held onto the side and pulled herself up on her tiptoes to peer inside. "Oh!"

"'Oh,' indeed." Michael smiled. "Do you want to play a game?"

Scott leaned over to Eric. "Yes, thermonuclear war." Eric grimaced, "What, too soon?"

Eric and Darryl chuckled.

Gabriel was already trying to get into the Vid-doc nearest him. John lifted the door and gave him a boost. "I want to play!"

Alexis narrowed her eyes for a split second.

"There are options?" Gabriel asked.

His exclamation stole Alexis' thought. Suddenly interested, she pulled herself up the side of the Vid-doc with some difficulty.

Michael offered his hands as a step when her foot slipped, but she waved him off and clambered up. She sat astride the lip of the Vid-doc as though it were a mountain she'd conquered and flopped over onto the soft pad inside. "I can do it by myself. See?"

Michael smiled and reached for the door, hesitating a moment before he closed it. "Just remember, you will feel pain during the game. Be aware of your surroundings at all times."

The twins laughed as one.

"Don't be silly, Daddy," Alexis told him. She activated the game menu and began to scroll through the options Gabriel had been so excited about a minute ago.

Gabriel lay back as John shut the Vid-doc door. His muffled little boy voice called, "Dinosaur Island? Alexis, let's play that one first!"

Alexis selected the option on her menu. "Let's do this!"

Annex Gate, Repurposed Leath Ship heading to Yoll System

Tabitha looked behind her, eyebrow raised. "And we had to spend hours crawling through this Gate line *because...*"

Bethany Anne sighed. "*Because*—for the hundredth time—if we Gated straight to Yoll from High Tortuga, any shady little pirate or anti-Federation fuckwit with the right equipment could follow the trail straight back to the place where my children are."

Tabitha huffed impatiently. "I am aware of that. I just want to be done with this already." The clearance to cross came through just then, and Tabitha whooped. "At *last*! I thought we were going to die of old age before we got out of here, and my lady bits would dry up."

"As if," Gabrielle smirked.

The Leath ship emerged on the Yollin side of the Gate, and Tabitha groaned loudly when she saw the slow-moving queue they were about to join. "Oh, just kill me now. I mean it! I'd rather die a quick and painless death than spend the rest of my life wasting away on this ship waiting for whatever the fuck it is that we're waiting for."

She turned to Bethany Anne. "What *are* we waiting for?"

"For me to be informed of your arrival," Meredith chimed from the speaker. "Welcome home, my Queen."

Bethany Anne smiled warmly. "It's good to hear your voice, Meredith. It's good to be home, even if just for a little while."

"It's wonderful to have you here. Will you allow me to bring you in?"

"Of course." Bethany Anne pushed back from the con, and the ship rose up out of the long line and sped straight toward the center of the Empire she'd built from nothing except her will, her friends, and plenty of gumption.

And some alien technology.

Meredith brought them into Bethany Anne's private dock, unused since her departure. They took what they needed from the ship and made their way to Bethany Anne's transfer room.

Gabrielle looked around as they crossed to the

hallway which would take them to Bethany Anne's personal quarters, which had also been sealed on her departure. "It's a little weird being back here. So many memories."

Jean snorted. "We've only been gone for a few years."

"That's why it's weird," Gabrielle protested. "It's like all that time this place was the heart of everything, and the base feels like…"

Tabitha put a finger to Gabrielle's mouth. "Let me stop you right there before you make a huge mistake. If you say 'another world,' I'll puke."

Gabrielle rolled her eyes. "So dramatic. I was going to say 'another lifetime.'"

Bethany Anne had to agree with that. It *was* another lifetime, just the latest she was living in a long succession of them. Was she still the same woman who had faced her mortality in a doctor's office on Earth some two hundred years ago and told inevitability to go fuck itself? She thought she was, at the core.

As for the rest?

Change happened, and you had to roll with it.

High Tortuga, Space Fleet Base, Immersive Recreation and Training Scenario, Dinosaur Island

Alexis and Gabriel found themselves in a rough hut made out of plant materials. Alexis glanced around, dismissed the empty space, and went straight for the door. She pulled back when she touched the handle.

Gabriel, I felt *that.* She rushed outside and knelt to touch the ground. *I can feel this, too.*

Gabriel shrugged. *So? This is virtual reality. It makes sense that we would be able to interact with stuff.*

Dad said we would feel pain. I wonder how much we can be hurt. Slap me.

Gabriel rolled his eyes and hit her across the face with a ringing slap. He knew better than to argue with his twin when she had that focused look.

Her eyes opened, and she drew a hand to her face. "Not *that* hard!"

Gabriel snickered and quoted, "'Word positioning is important.'"

"You're an ass," she complained, rubbing her stinging cheek.

Gabriel's eyes widened. "You're really hurt?" He slapped himself across the face just as hard. "Ow!"

Alexis rolled her eyes. "No nuance whatsoever."

Gabriel didn't hear her. He'd already wandered off to explore the area around the hut.

Alexis looked around. The jungle was almost familiar but different enough from the environment she was used to that it gave her a slight chill.

Gabriel paused with his hand on a tree and looked back at Alexis. "I wonder if we can get eaten?"

"Maybe I'll get lucky and you can tell me?" Alexis snarked. She followed him into the tree line hesitantly. "Here's a thought… What if Dad transported us to the southern continent?"

"He wouldn't do that. Don't worry." He looked around and saw a faint path cut into the undergrowth. "Come on, this way."

Gabriel's hand found hers, and they set off into the

jungle.

Eric and Scott winced when Gabriel slapped Alexis.

"I can't believe you thought of this," Scott told Michael.

Michael threw a piece of popcorn into his mouth and smirked as he chewed. "I figure it's got to be worth a few years' entertainment at least."

John and Darryl returned with a couple of extra chairs from another room, and they all returned to watching the events unfold on the screen wall.

The children walked hand-in-hand into the jungle.

"They look so small," Darryl commented.

Michael flashed him a wolfish grin. "Don't be fooled by their size. My children are nobody's easy pickings, even at this young age." He looked back at the screen. "Although... they haven't made the best start."

"What do you mean?" John asked.

"They've taken the right path." Michael shook his head. "But they missed the instructions."

John raised an eyebrow, still watching Alexis and Gabriel's progress through the jungle. A herd of small dinosaurs came into view up ahead.

Scott, Darryl, and Eric turned as one to Michael.

"You guys need to watch," Michael told them. "I'm going to send one of you in as a consultant to advise... when it's time."

John dragged his gaze from the screen. "When will that be?"

Michael settled back to watch. "After their first deaths."

CHAPTER TWELVE

QBBS *Meredith Reynolds*, Bethany Anne's Personal Quarters

The General was waiting in the sitting room when Bethany Anne transported the four of them in. "Okay, now it's weird." She looked around at her old life and felt a pang of something she didn't want to examine too closely at the moment. She shook her head and held her arms out to her father. "Hi, Dad."

Lance hugged her tightly. "It's so good to see you, sweetheart. How are my grandchildren?"

"Wow, not even a segue." Tabitha snickered at Lance's now-red face and waved for him to continue. "I'm kidding. Go ahead, get mushy. I need a shower and some clean clothes." She grabbed her luggage in one hand and took it through to the bedroom. Lance looked at a suspiciously long and boxy bag she was carrying. "Is that…"

Tabitha held up a finger without turning around or stopping. "Leave Gracie out of it."

Lance looked at Bethany Anne, nonplussed.

Jean rolled her eyes. "It's a big-ass rifle she took off a Shrillexian in a bar fight on Devon."

Lance's confusion deepened. "I thought it was called High Tortuga now?"

Bethany Anne shook her head. "No, that's old Devon. Jean's talking about New Devon, which we're just calling Devon since that's the whole point of taking the planet over."

Lance rubbed his forehead. "I'm sure it will all make sense soon enough."

Jean and Gabrielle excused themselves, leaving Bethany Anne and her father alone in the sitting room to talk. Lance raised his eyebrows.

Bethany Anne rolled her eyes. "The twins are great, Dad. You only spoke to them a couple of weeks ago."

They chatted for a while, catching each other up on the little details of life that were best exchanged in person. Tabitha joined them a short time later, followed by Jean soon after that.

Bethany Anne stood as Gabrielle returned with her hair wrapped in a towel. "Please tell me you didn't use the last towel?"

Gabrielle grinned and shook her head. "Plenty left for you."

Lance was distracted by an insistent beeping from his wrist. He looked down and made a pained face. "Sorry, ladies. I have to get on a video conference."

Bethany Anne craned to see what he was looking at. "Oh, yeah? Is it something to do with the problem you've been having?"

Lance pulled his sleeve over his wrist before Bethany Anne could see anything useful and leaned over to kiss her on the top of her head. "I'll tell you after dinner tonight. And no, I don't need you to butt in." He ignored her pout. "Just don't take too long getting there, Patricia has been clattering around for days making... You know, I'm not sure. She hasn't stayed still long enough to tell me."

High Tortuga, Space Fleet Base, Immersive Recreation and Training Scenario, Dinosaur Island

The foliage thickened steadily as Gabriel and Alexis pushed farther into the jungle. More than once they debated turning around, but each time they chose to press on and see where the path led. After what felt like an age but was more like a couple of hours, the twins noticed that the path widened some ahead.

Alexis pointed out signs of nearby animal activity— roughed-up bark on a tree here, a stripped bush there. "I wonder if we need to eat while we're in here?"

Gabriel stopped to consider. He eventually shrugged. "I guess we'll find out if we get hungry, won't we?"

Alexis nodded and continued walking.

Gabriel followed her, keeping watch all around them. He spotted movement through a break in the foliage to the side of the path. "Hey, Alexis, look!"

Alexis followed Gabriel's finger to a small clearing where a herd of pint-sized dinosaurs was busily stripping the leaves from the lower branches of the trees. "Oh, they're so sweet!"

Gabriel started to go closer to get a better look. The

dinosaurs turned orange lizard eyes on Gabriel the moment his foot strayed from the path.

Alexis grabbed his arm and pulled him back. "Stay on the path."

Gabriel looked at the dinosaurs warily as they went back to cropping. "Yeah, you've got it."

They continued down the path a while until they came to the crest of a gentle rise. The twins stopped to look out over the rolling expanse of the game biome.

The jungle stretched as far as they could see. It was broken only by the pale blue line of a large body of water in the far distance, and a looming mountain off to the west. The path split at the top of the hill, giving them a choice of directions.

Alexis shared a concerned glance with her brother. "I think it's time to get some help."

Gabriel nodded. "Phyrro?"

The voice came from all around them. "Access denied."

The twins looked at each other.

That wasn't Phyrro.

Alexis sighed. *I know that.*

"Why can't we talk to Phyrro?" she demanded of the voice.

"The system you are requesting has been locked out due to an inability to connect on this technologically deficient world."

Gabriel frowned. "Meaning?"

"Meaning Daddy is a complete pain in the ass." She stamped her foot and stormed down the path leading to the mountain. "Come on, we'll figure this out by ourselves."

CHAPTER THIRTEEN

The black teardrop spun like a bullet through the void, a trail of twisted and pitted metals, ice, and rock tumbling in its silent wake.

The leading edge of the alien structure had been polished smooth by the constant barrage of minute particles traveling in the opposite direction at superspeed. The trailing end was made up of the smaller shards that continually came loose from the sides. Most were gathered by the slipstream and thrown into the vortex at the tail. From a distance, it could easily be mistaken for a massive comet.

Which was precisely the point.

A harder collision carved a slightly larger chunk from the rough teardrop and sent it spinning out into the vacuum. The alien structure slowed, shattering the illusion that it was a mere ice ball. A nest of long cables snaked out from the rear and pulled the dislodged chunk—a hollowed-out Leath battle cruiser—back to the main bulk.

An active Gate appeared a few hundred kilometers away. The cables retracted while the mass of wrecks adjusted its trajectory, picked up speed, and vanished through the Gate.

Yollin Sector, QBBS *Meredith Reynolds*

"Mommy, look at *meeeee!* Faster, Bethany Anne, *faster!*" Little Kevin squealed with delight as Bethany Anne stood beneath him with her hands raised to give him her own special version of an airplane. He was red-faced and grinning, his arms spread out as he made wide, seemingly unsupported laps of the room.

Bethany Anne glanced at Patricia, who nodded and held her thumb and forefinger a fraction of an inch apart. She increased the speed of the Etheric energy loop she had created to fly her baby brother around a touch.

Kevin's feet kicked with glee. "Wheeeeee!"

"Sure beats the usual way of doing it," Patricia remarked to Gabrielle.

"This is nothing," Gabrielle told her. "When Stephen and JM were nine, I found her doing this with them in one of the hangars." She made a face at the memory. "She made *full* use of the space. I walked in to see my boys thirty feet up in the air."

Bethany Anne snickered as she brought Kevin back down to the floor. "They loved it, Eric thought it was hilarious. You were the only one who had a problem, if I remember."

Gabrielle narrowed her eyes.

Patricia paled. She held her arms out for Kevin, who was yawning after all the excitement. "Come on, sleepy-head. Time for your nap."

Kevin looked at his mother as though she'd just stolen his world. "But, Moooom! Bethany Anne is here! And Aunt Tabbie promised me stories!"

Tabitha grinned at Patricia and shrugged. "I did promise the little tyke some stories." She turned to Kevin, whose eyes were filling up. "I'll take you to your room and tell you a story now, but you have to nap afterward, okay? You can show me all the cool stuff you have."

The impending storm on Kevin's face disappeared without a trace, and he let out another yawn. "Okay, then."

Patricia gaped. "Tabitha, you live here now." She held up a hand to answer Tabitha's look. "No arguing. My boy has never agreed to take a nap in his life." She knelt and kissed Kevin. "Love you, sweetie. Be good for Aunt Tabitha."

Kevin smiled sweetly. "Yes, Mommy." He fitted his hand into Tabitha's and led her from the room, chattering the whole way.

Bethany Anne watched them go with a smile. She'd gone through a phase of wishing she had a little brother once upon a time. Someone to look out for and boss around had been her thinking back then.

Kevin may have come along too late for any of that, but it was so good to be home. To hold the boy in her arms and spend real time playing with him.

Patricia interrupted Bethany Anne's thoughts. "Tabitha is amazing with Kevin."

Bethany Anne nodded. "Kids have always loved her. She

has a gift." As many rough edges as Tabitha had, she couldn't be faulted for the tenderness she showed toward the children. "She's the same with Alexis and Gabriel. The twins worship the ground she walks on."

Jean came in with a tray of snacks. "What are we talking about?"

Gabrielle leaned over and took a cookie when Jean put the tray on the table. "How great Tabitha is with little ones."

Jean raised an eyebrow and chuckled. "Yeah, but just watch her suitability as a role model plummet once they're teenagers. That's all I'm saying."

Gabrielle snickered. "I wonder how Michael is getting on by himself with the terrible twosome?"

Bethany Anne shrugged and snagged a brownie. "Either he's doing just fine, or they're…"

Jean and Gabrielle were quick to jump in.

Gabrielle went first. "Mind-reading their father to wrap him around their fingers?"

Jean followed with, "Escaping into the Etheric?"

Gabrielle shrugged. "Making pets out of the local wildlife?"

Jean smirked. "Setting the base on fire?"

Patricia put a hand to her mouth and giggled. "Oh, my! What active imaginations you have! I'm sure it won't be all that bad."

Bethany Anne fixed her stepmom with a serious look. "No, it could be even *worse*. All those things actually happened in the last six months."

Jean snorted into her coffee. "And *then* some."

"And there was me, complaining that Kevin fusses over his nap." Patricia shook her head. "Although I will say, your brother has a stubborn streak a mile wide. I can't think where he gets that from."

Bethany Anne grinned. "Wait until he brings back something like a four-foot boa constrictor and tells you its name is Huggy." She turned to Gabrielle. "It was Huggy, right?"

"Who cares?" Gabrielle shuddered. "That monster was *not* a snake. Snakes don't make eye contact and salivate when you walk into the room."

Patricia grimaced. "Sounds dreadful, sweetheart. Makes me glad that Lance and I didn't pass that level of enhancement onto Kevin. While he is stronger and smart for his age, we're not having any adventures like that with him."

She crossed her fingers mentally that the situation remained the same. "So, how advanced are the twins now? Your father tells me that they're developing abilities with the Etheric already. How are you both coping with *that*?"

"Mmmhmm." Bethany Anne nodded and finished chewing the mouthful of brownie while she thought it over. "It's a challenge, I'll admit. Michael and I agree that they need to be trained to prevent another accidental crossing like they did on their birthday."

"But they're only three years old," Patricia fretted. "Should they be training so young?"

"They're nothing like three-year-olds." Bethany Anne smirked. "Besides, we're making it a game for them. Look, we're not going to stay on High Tortuga forever, and there will always be assholes who would attack them to hurt me.

We're not your conventional family, so raising them the conventional way would be failing them as parents. This way they're prepared for whatever comes." She thought for a moment. "Well, as well as we can."

Patricia still wasn't convinced. "Yes, but they're still toddlers, even if they don't look or act like it. How are they handling this 'training?'"

Bethany Anne raised her eyebrows a couple of times, a smile splitting her face. "Like a pair of badass Reynolds kids, of course. How else?"

High Tortuga, Space Fleet Base, Michael's Office, Vid-Doc Room

Michael slapped the top of Eric's arm and pointed at the screen. "Here comes some fun." He tossed some popcorn into his mouth and offered the bowl to the others. The screen still showed Alexis and Gabriel, who were having an encounter with some small dinosaurs. Gabriel had spotted them through the foliage and moved to investigate.

Scott took the bowl. "What fun?"

"If they leave the path, they trigger a game event," Michael revealed.

"What kind of event?" John asked.

Michael grinned. "Nothing too big at this early stage." He looked a little disappointed when Alexis pulled Gabriel back. "Just a little taste of what's to come that would have given them an advantage later in the game." He shrugged. "No matter. If they miss the next one, I will send one of you in to assist."

"What are they doing?" Eric pointed at the screen. Alexis and Gabriel had stopped at a fork in the path.

Michael turned the volume up, and they heard the children calling for their EI.

Phyrro's voice came from the speaker. "The children are calling, and I cannot reach them."

Michael held a finger up. "Alexis and Gabriel are learning self-sufficiency, Phyrro. They will not always have access to EIs and AIs to guide them through the decision-making process. See, they're thinking about their options."

The twins were stalled at the fork.

Darryl frowned. "Which path do they need to take?"

"They will take the route to the mountain," Michael told him. "The game is designed to lead them to the next stage, and Alexis would never choose the sea."

"What if Gabriel takes the lead?" Darryl asked.

Michael raised an eyebrow at him. "Do you even *know* my children?" As if to prove his point, Alexis took charge and demanded to know why they couldn't speak to Phyrro.

"Daddy is a complete pain in the ass." Alexis stormed down the path to the mountain as the guys cracked up at her outburst.

"I did *not* teach them that," Michael told them as he pointed to the screen. "That was all Bethany Anne."

"She sounded *just* like BA," John managed through his tears of laughter.

"Come *on*, Gabriel!" Alexis pushed ahead to get to the top of the next rise.

Gabriel decided it was safer to remain a few paces behind his sister until her temper passed. "I don't see why Dad thought it would be a fun game without Phyrro to help."

Alexis snorted. "Who said it wasn't fun?"

"This isn't like any game I've played before." Gabriel spread his hands out to indicate the surrounding jungle. "It's got no purpose. What are we supposed to do, just walk through the jungle endlessly?"

Alexis stopped in her tracks. "You're right, I think we missed something." She clenched her fists and stamped her feet. "It's too late to go back *now*."

They climbed to the top of the rise and stopped to choose their route through the valley below.

"Look." Gabriel pointed at a clearing at the bottom of the valley, where a mixed group of dinosaurs was drinking from a long pool. "They look like plant-eaters."

"Herbivores," Alexis supplied.

"Walking thesaurus," Gabriel shot back. He began working his way down the scree-covered slope, using the trees to keep his speed down. "Come on, I want to get a closer look."

Alexis gave him a doubtful look but followed just the same.

John turned his head to Michael. "*Are* they herbivores?"

Michael nodded. "Those ones are, yes."

Darryl, Scott, and Eric exchanged glances.

John kept watching with his arms folded, assessing the

whole time. "They're gonna be in the shit if they keep that up," he remarked.

The twins crashed through the foliage at the edge of the pool, startling the smaller dinosaurs into scampering away.

Gabriel dashed over to a long and moderately large dinosaur with a line of bony plates along its spine. "Alexis, it's a dragon!"

Alexis remained by the tree line. "If it is a dragon, then where are its wings?"

"Oh, yeah." Gabriel looked downcast for a moment but brightened when he put a hand on the dinosaur's side and it didn't immediately move away. "Shall we ride them? Maybe we shouldn't. Mom wasn't messing around when she told Dad we weren't to go near any dinosaurs."

"Well, *technically* they're not real dinosaurs, so we wouldn't be breaking Mom's rules." Alexis still hesitated. "I don't know…"

Gabriel was already scrambling up the dinosaur's side. Alexis sighed and threw up her hands. "I suppose we'll get to the mountain a lot faster if we're not walking. Now, how do you steer a dinosaur?"

"I don't know, ask it?" Gabriel shinnied along the neck until he came eye to eye with the dinosaur, who had just noticed the tiny human for the first time.

Its eye flew wide in alarm, and it shook its head to remove Gabriel from its neck. Gabriel clung tightly and whooped. The other dinosaurs lifted their heads, spooked by the noise. They stopped drinking and began a stampede to get away from the pool.

Alexis danced and dodged around to avoid being crushed by the fleeing feet. "Gabriel, get *down* from there!"

Out of nowhere, Gabriel's steed was tumbled to the ground by another dinosaur, a raptor-looking predator that was a little larger than the peaceful plant eater. Gabriel dived from its head and landed in a roll to avoid being crushed.

Alexis screamed when the raptor tore the throat out of the herbivore and splashed her with blood. She shook her hands rapidly to get it off. "Ugh, Gabriel! It's slimy! And *hot*!"

Gabriel grabbed her hand and pulled her under a large bush. "Yeah, well, we're going to be dead if we don't get out of here. Look, there are more."

Alexis followed his finger and saw the rest of the raptor pack coming at them. "Follow the herd, quick! Run!"

They pelted hand-in-hand into the undergrowth, dashing between the legs of the larger dinosaurs to put some distance—and some prey—between themselves and the predators.

It was carnage. The meat-eating pack tore into the herd with abandon. However, the larger herbivores were no easy meal. They fought back, churning up the ground beneath them as they stamped and reared to shake their attackers off.

Alexis had never run so fast in her life. She felt her brother's hand grip hers tightly, matching her pace as the dinosaurs warred around them. They ducked a long tail that swooped low across their path and dodged the snapping jaws of one of the raptors when it got a little too close. Gabriel pulled her out of the path of a falling dinosaur and dragged her onward before any of the raptors who were piling onto the wounded beast noticed the two bite-sized humans.

They were both breathing hard, but they didn't let the burn in their chests stop them from fleeing.

I'm so tired! Alexis panted even in their minds. *How are we feeling this?*

Gabriel grunted, shooting a quick glance over his shoulder. *Not the time, sis. Just run!*

John raised an eyebrow at Michael. "Now?"

Michael nodded. "Just lie down in the Vid-doc, and I'll pipe you in."

"No funny business, okay?" He got in and eyed Michael before he pulled the door closed. "Okay, I'm done reading through the objectives. Send me in."

Michael smirked when Eve came into the room just as he input the commands to insert John into the game. Eve walked over to the console and looked up at the screen, where John had just appeared a little ways from the children.

A matching smirk appeared on her face.

John sprinted through the stampede until he reached the twins. He scooped one child under each arm and worked his way out of the crush. When a few raptors saw them separate and moved to circle them, John's eyes flashed red. He snarled and *pushed* a thick wave of fear.

The raptors halted and tilted their heads at John. He held Alexis and Gabriel close and glared at the dinosaurs. One put a clawed foot forward, testing. John snarled at them again, a deep and rumbling promise of death to any raptor that took a step closer.

The raptors were bright enough to understand the threat. They blinked in the realization that they were not the apex predators in this situation and backed off to refocus their efforts on more timid prey.

"What was that?" Gabriel asked John. His voice trembled a bit, but the interest component was stronger. "They were scared. Can I do that?"

John shrugged. "I don't know, can you?"

He put the children down now that the danger had passed. They clung to his legs, still a little shaken by the sudden excitement.

Alexis was first to recover. "Uncle John, we got distracted and missed the instructions."

John smiled and took a knee on the ground between them. He wrapped an arm around each child. "I don't have long before your dad pulls me out again, so listen up while I give you both some pointers..."

Eve turned to Michael, the less-than-altruistic grin still on her face. "So you're giving them their first taste?"

Scott, Darryl, and Eric had been watching the events on the screen unfold with something between awe and horror.

"You did this?" Scott asked incredulously.

Eve gave him a flat look. "Of course. Who else knows

this technology like I do? It was my specialty back on Earth, even with the horrible electronics I had to deal with. This is my best work ever."

Darryl frowned. "What's that mean?"

She looked up at the screen again. "It means they'd best hope they don't get bitten."

CHAPTER FOURTEEN

High Tortuga, Space Fleet Base, Security Pit

An alarm went off in the quiet of the graveyard shift, startling Jennifer and Charles almost out of their skins.

"It's an unidentified...something," Charles shouted over the klaxon.

"What do you mean, 'something?'" Jennifer looked at Charles and then down at her monitor. "CEREBRO, shut that damn alarm off. Then identify whatever set the damn thing off."

"That's a lot of damns," Charles teased.

The klaxon cut out and a moment later a fuzzy image came up on Jennifer's screen. "Resolve."

The image sharpened, revealing...nothing.

"What the hell?"

"We are receiving a communication," CEREBRO told them.

"Put it onscreen, please."

The screen went black, then came back to life with the

face of Addix, the Ixtali spymistress. "Good evening. Would you please ask CEREBRO to cease pointing the planetary defense system at me? Lady does not appreciate the gesture, either." Her mandibles indicated that she was merely teasing and wasn't actually offended.

Jennifer was still mortified. "Of course, Spymistress. We weren't expecting you. I'm so sorry."

Addix waved her off. "Just contact Michael and inform him of my arrival."

Above High Tortuga, *The Lady Princess*

Addix left her personal quarters and made her way back to the bridge. It was a lot simpler to walk the narrow passages of the ship without the bulky robes she used to wear snagging on every protrusion she passed.

Of course, she would still wear the robes in public. This new confidence in herself was for her and those who had helped her to gain it alone. To everyone else she was just another Ixtali, one of many. Her role was not to stand out from the crowd, since notoriety would be an endless complication—and that was definitely *not* how Addix worked.

She preferred the freedom of anonymity. If she were instantly recognizable wherever she went, it would cut her off from many of the tricks of her trade, making her a much less effective spy.

Lady spoke through the speaker as Addix entered the bridge. "You have a call."

Addix's mandibles twitched. "No snark today?"

Lady sighed. "I cannot believe they were going to fry me. I would rather not discuss it. Your call is ready."

Eve came up on the screen. It was fairly easy to read human moods, but Eve gave nothing away. Addix found the smooth lines of the android's face more than a little disconcerting. She also had her suspicions about Eve's status as an EI. She'd noticed more than a few snippets of what sounded like opinion from her over the last three years. However, she'd also learned about Eve's close guard over her privacy, and also her propensity for pulling wicked pranks when she felt slighted.

"I was expecting Michael."

Eve tilted her head. "He's busy with the children's training."

Addix's mandibles twitched in excitement. "Has it begun?"

Eve nodded. "It has. I can take a message if it's urgent."

Addix shook her head. It was strange how one picked up these human gestures over the years. "It will wait. I'd rather tell him in person."

Yollin Sector, QBBS *Meredith Reynolds*, Bethany Anne's Personal Quarters

"Brunette or redhead?" Tabitha held the wigs up one at a time, grinning wickedly at the horrified expression on Jean's face.

Gabrielle selected a few items of Torcellan clothing from the rack and grabbed the elaborate wig Tabitha offered. "Do we have the right makeup?"

Bethany Anne pointed to an industrial-looking case on wheels. "One reverse spray tan coming right up."

Gabrielle sat still for Bethany Anne to apply the makeup.

Jean shook her head, threw a voluminous hooded robe over what she was already wearing, and picked up a prop breathing mask to cover the lower part of her face. "I'm thinking I'd rather go completely incognito than go through all of *that*." She pointed at the elaborate Torcellan hairpiece Gabrielle was planning to wear with disgust. "Especially *that*. Fuck, no." She rummaged in one of the boxes of disguise elements scattered around the anteroom and came up with a pair of wobbly gel somethings. "What the hell are *these* for?"

Bethany Anne looked over from doing Gabrielle's makeup and made a face at them. "Beats the fuck out of me." She shrugged and scooped another blob of the thick alabaster foundation from the palette she was holding.

Gabrielle winced as Bethany Anne applied the cold sponge to her face. "It will be something or other designed to enhance your body."

Tabitha looked up from the box she was searching and grinned. "They're helping hands for the less bootylicious." She laughed at the blank looks she was getting and patted her ass before she returned to digging through the box. "Can't all be as gifted in the rear aspect as I am."

"Ew." Jean dropped the gel pads back in the box with a grimace. "Yeah, I'll give those a pass."

Gabrielle rolled her eyes and walked over to the clothes rack to get what she needed to complete her transformation. "What are you doing?"

Bethany Anne snickered. "I think I'll skip all of that." She concentrated and her face changed into something just different enough, even as her skin became more golden in hue and her eyes changed to a deep, warm brown. "Well, what do I look like?"

Tabitha turned to look and did a double take. "Oh, now that's just weird."

Bethany Anne frowned. "What?"

"You look like my older, hotter sister." Tabitha scowled. "No fair. Now I've got to do something spectacular." She hastily swapped out the disguise she'd chosen, secured her double-armload of items, and swept out of the room.

Bethany Anne's mouth fell open. "Older?"

Jean sighed and rolled her eyes. "So dramatic."

Tabitha breezed back in shortly afterward, completely unrecognizable with the blue makeup she'd applied to every visible inch of her skin.

Gabrielle returned soon after that wearing her Torcellan getup. "I can see why they're so vain about their hair." She ran a hand over the heavy wig. "The real thing would take a lot of upkeep."

Tabitha snickered, then looked longingly at Gracie's case. "I'll be back," she whispered to the gun.

"Do you and the rifle need a little time alone?" Bethany Anne asked. "We can leave you two alone and hit the stores without you."

Tabitha grinned. "Nope, all good, thanks. Now, are we going to get some retail therapy, or what?"

Lance entered Bethany Anne's quarters. "Meredith, have I missed them?"

"You have," Meredith replied.

Lance sighed. "Dammit, I wanted to catch them before they left. I hope they stay under the radar. I'd hate to require Bethany Anne to wipe someone."

"I can help watch over them," Meredith offered.

Lance nodded. "I think that would be best."

QBBS *Meredith Reynolds*, Level 00, Open Court

"So, a human, a Torcellan, a…" she waved a hand in Tabitha's direction, "and a whatever the fuck Jean is pretending to be—"

"Hey!" Jean objected.

"A whatever the fuck Jean is pretending to be," Bethany Anne repeated, "Walk into a bar… Dammit!" She shrugged and pushed open the door of the boutique. "I lost the punchline."

Bethany Anne inhaled the smell of new shoe leather as she looked around the little slice of heaven. "Oh, for the sweet love of all that is…" She headed straight for the lit display cases at the back of the store where the exclusive lines were kept.

The sales clerk, a cute young human with bouncy curls and a bouncier step, came straight over. "Hi, can I help you ladies find what you're looking for?"

Bethany Anne smiled and pointed at the display. "I'll try those, those, and…those too."

The sales clerk bent to pull the relevant boxes from the

drawers under the display unit. "A woman with taste, I like it. what size do you take?"

Bethany Anne smirked. "A seven."

The clerk grinned. "Really? You wear the same size as the Empress. You're so lucky!"

Bethany Anne took the box the clerk held out. "Oh? Why does that make me lucky?"

The clerk stood with the other three boxes. "Because it's considered the perfect size. Also, her shoe obsession is pretty famous. One visit from Bethany Anne could make the year for a small business like this. All the shoe stores make sure to stock her size in case she ever comes to shop."

Bethany Anne smiled and glanced over the display again. "Well, let's see if we can make this into one of those days for you."

Jean laughed in Bethany Anne's mind.

Bethany Anne fixed her with a stare. *I don't know why you're laughing. You're going to build me somewhere to keep all of these. I don't want my little splurge getting back to Michael.*

"A little splurge, you said." Jean's tone was pure disbelief as she watched the line of antigrav pallets head off to the storage cube they'd brought with them. "You're definitely going to need an extension to your secret lair."

They wandered along the concourse, taking their time to browse the stores. Tabitha stopped here and there to sample the food from the vendors they passed. She nibbled on her corndog, making little noises as she ate. "Mmm, real Earth food."

Gabrielle wrinkled her nose. "I don't think street vendors are the way to go. You couldn't hold out until we found a place for lunch?"

Tabitha stuck her tongue out at Gabrielle. "You're not still sore about those tacos on Devon, are you?"

Gabrielle rolled her eyes and hurried to catch up with Bethany Anne. "It's changed a lot here."

Bethany Anne nodded. "You're not wrong. But look around us." She nodded toward the busy concourse and continued mentally, *More peoples are able to exist in harmony since I stepped down and my dad took over. He's done a great job of growing the Federation. It doesn't need me.*

Gabrielle laid a hand on her arm. *Stepping down was the best decision—for you, as well as for the Federation.*

Bethany Anne shrugged. *There's only so much political bullshit one woman can take. Besides, you know they did me a favor. How else was I supposed to get out of here? Running an empire was only ever going to get in the way of what we left Earth to do.*

Tabitha chimed in, *Killing the fucking Kurtherians?*

Bethany Anne grinned. *Got it in one. After all these long years, we're finally almost ready to take the fight to them instead of running around the galaxy stamping out the wars they create after the fact.* She sniffed, catching a rich aroma she hadn't had the pleasure of smelling for a while. "Italian for lunch, ladies?"

Jean nodded.

"Oh, yes," Gabrielle agreed.

Tabitha finished the last of her corndog and threw the wrapper in a nearby trashcan. "I could go for lasagna."

They tracked down the source of the deliciousness. It was a tiny place almost hidden between two larger, much busier eating establishments, neither of which smelled half as good as the cozy bistro. Bethany Anne led them inside, where they were greeted warmly and seated by the owner.

"What's good?" Tabitha asked without raising her head from the menu.

"All our food is cooked from scratch using fresh ingredients, so I tell my customers that if they want a culinary experience they've come to the right place." He gave them a rueful smile. "However, I must tell you that food here takes a little while longer than the places on either side."

Bethany Anne leaned back in her chair. "How much longer?" She didn't mind waiting a little while if the food was worth it, but she didn't have the whole day.

Tabitha put her menu down. "Never mind how long it takes. I've already got my heart set on lasagna. Can you *smell* that sauce?" She almost wished she could take some for Ryu and Hirotoshi.

But then again, maybe it was best that she didn't. That way, she didn't have to admit that she meant well but then ate her gift en route back to High Tortuga.

CHAPTER FIFTEEN

High Tortuga, Space Fleet Base, Immersive Recreation and Training Scenario, Dinosaur Island

"So are you two good?" Alexis and Gabriel nodded. John stood and braced himself to return to his body. "Michael, I'm ready."

Nothing happened.

He tried again, a little louder in case they had the volume down out there. "Michael? You can get me out of here now."

The corner of Alexis' mouth twitched, and Gabriel snickered.

John tried to activate his HUD, but nothing happened. His brow furrowed. "Very funny, Michael. You had no intention of letting me out of this da...rned game, did you?"

"Does that mean you're going to play, too?" Alexis asked.

"Say yes, Uncle John!" Gabriel pleaded.

John sighed and tucked away his thoughts of revenge for later. "I guess your dad isn't giving me much choice, although it's always good to get some time with my favorite twins."

High Tortuga, Space Fleet Base, Michael's Office, Vid-Doc Room

Eric threw a handful of popcorn at John on the screen. "I won't tell his godsons that he said that."

Scott laughed. "I think Stephen and JM could handle it. They're not little kids."

Darryl came back from the bathroom and grabbed the popcorn from Eric on his way to his seat. "What did I miss?"

Michael put his feet back up after Darryl had passed. "Just John realizing he'd been played. Want me to play it back?"

Darryl grinned as he sat down. "Oh, hell yeah!"

The three clambered up the side of the steep valley. The children were out of breath again. At the top, they came to a stop against a half-embedded boulder and rested with their hands on their knees while they sucked in grateful lungsful of virtual air.

John folded his arms and looked around. The path was gone, and there was no discernible route through the thickening jungle from where he was standing. "What's the objective here?"

Alexis raised her eyebrows. "Uncle John, we didn't review the game objectives before we started."

Gabriel looked at his feet. "We were too excited to play the game."

John's shoulders dropped. He smiled at the twins and ruffled their heads. "Huh. Well, I guess I can't be upset about it if I didn't review them either. What did you learn from this?"

Gabriel gave the answer. "That we should always review the available information."

John nodded. "Anything else?"

The twins looked at each other, then at John with butter-wouldn't-melt expressions. "That sometimes the adults get it wrong too?" Alexis offered.

"You're right," John told her. He grinned at her incredulous expression and set off down the next slope into the trees. "Come on, we'll work it out as we go."

The children scrambled after him. "What if we go the wrong way?" Gabriel asked.

John looked back over his shoulder to make sure they were following. "Since your dad decided to mess with me, I think it's only fair to share what he gave away before he trapped me in here. We're heading for that mountain over there."

"I could have told you that. This place has an order to it."

"That's because your dad and Eve designed this game to lead you through the tasks."

Gabriel looked puzzled for a second, then dismissed any anxiety he may have had and plowed after John on the path he'd made.

Alexis stewed in consideration.

John noted the difference between the two, as he so often did. Gabriel was like a clear sky on a sunny day, where Alexis had depths even now that John couldn't fathom.

They walked for a while, with John clearing the path ahead for the children. The jungle soon began to press in closer on all sides.

"Time for a break, children." He paused a beat to let them catch up.

"Are we any closer to the mountain?" Alexis asked.

Alexis began to pace, tapping her lips with a finger in a way that gave John the shivers.

Nothing good ever came of that expression on her mother's face.

"This game can't be just about playing explorer. It's too big, and I still haven't worked out why we can *feel* everything." She turned dark, assessing eyes on John. "What else did Dad let slip? I just know he wouldn't be able to resist showing off a little."

John bit back his laughter. "I'm afraid he resisted this time, sweetie. Apart from our direction he gave me nothing."

Alexis rolled her eyes. "Great."

They were surrounded on all sides by a wall of green. Gabriel turned a slow circle. "Where are we?"

"Let's see." John glanced around, looking for a tree that was thick enough to support him. They grew too close together to grow outward, so they were mostly too slender for him to climb to the top and get a clue about their location.

Alexis worked out what he was doing and scampered over to shinny up one of the tall, thin trunks.

"Be careful up there," John called. "Remember, you can be hurt in here."

"I will," she replied. She dug her feet into the trunk and used her hands to pull herself up, just like on the ropes in physical training. She scrunched her eyes shut against the glare of the sun as her head broke through the canopy.

The rays were warm, and the wind danced around her. Alexis wondered how she could feel so refreshed by the sensation when she wasn't really here. She knew Eve had something to do with it because the EI and her father had been secretly planning this for weeks.

They thought she didn't know, but she'd caught a glimpse here and there when his mind was in one of its rare unguarded moments—which usually happened when her mother walked into the room.

"What can you see?" Uncle John's voice reached her from below.

Alexis snapped her attention back to the task at hand and brought her hand up to her eyes to shade them from the strong afternoon sun. She located the mountain and scrambled back down the tree trunk.

John was waiting with outstretched arms when she got back near to the ground. He put her down gently, and she pointed in the direction they needed to take. "This way."

Eric peered in at the windows in the Vid-Doc doors one at a time. John and the twins appeared to be sleeping peacefully, belying the effort of the grueling trek they were making on the screen. He turned back to the room. "So they're not being hurt physically?"

Eve shook her head. "No. The Vid-Doc is implanting the reality directly into their brains, playing their central nervous systems like a harp."

Scott turned from the screen. "A harp?"

"A sufficient analogy." She walked over to the empty Vid-Doc and gestured for Scott and Eric to come and take a look.

Darryl came over and stuck his head inside, leaving Michael alone to watch the children and John. "It looks like an ordinary Pod-doc."

Eve inclined her head. "It's pretty much the same as the Pod-doc setup. It was just a question of repurposing the machinery and recalibrating the programming to create an authentic sensory experience."

"And the children need to feel pain, why?" Scott asked. "It's a little intense for a game. Just sayin.'"

Michael chose not to answer.

Eve smiled. "Training. This method is superior, especially considering where the lessons are leading."

She lifted a shoulder. "You know how it is. No pain, no gain."

The forest eventually thinned out into grassland. John kept his eye on the children while they ran ahead, energized by the sudden freedom of movement that leaving the jungle behind provided.

They held out their hands to be tickled by the waist-high grass as they ran. John looked up as if there was a camera above him somewhere. "I hope you're getting good video of this for Bethany Anne. She loves this stuff." He caught himself looking up and shook his head. "Just keep that bit to yourselves."

The grassland continued on for a ways. They passed the odd herd of grass-eating dinosaurs, but the crossing was otherwise uneventful until they reached the tree-lined bank of a fast-flowing river.

Alexis and Gabriel stood side by side in the shade of an overhanging tree, looking at the river between them and the mountain in the not-too-far distance. "I think we found the next challenge, Uncle John."

Gabriel looked up at John. "Should we try to swim across it?"

Alexis paled. "No way. We don't even know what's in there. We might get eaten!"

"Don't look at me. It's your game, I'm just the muscle." John sat on a boulder, folded his arms, and left them to work out a solution.

A short time later they had cobbled together a raft from an assortment of tree trunks and vines, combined with a fair amount of sweat and repressed cursing from John.

Alexis stood back, finally satisfied with the raft's sturdiness. She eyed the river warily. "I'm still worried there might be something waiting in the water."

Gabriel had similar concerns. "Well, we have to cross, or we can't get to the mountain." He pointed at a herd of small, feathery dinosaurs near the water's edge. "They're there. They look like ducks. What if we shoo them into the water and see what happens?"

Alexis nodded and they ran to the water's edge, waving their arms. The duck-dinos took to the water, screeching their displeasure at the perceived threat.

The three watched the duck-dinos bobbing across the river. No creature from the deep rose to snatch them. Gabriel waited until they reached the other bank and made to give the raft a shove. "I think we can just go."

Alexis looked up at John, who shrugged. "Now's as good a time as any."

They maneuvered the makeshift raft to the water's edge, and John held it steady while Alexis and Gabriel climbed on. He pushed it out into the water and held onto the back while he kicked to propel them to the other side of the river.

Alexis wrapped her arms around her knees. "I'm so glad you're super-strong, Uncle John."

John chuckled through a faceful of water and kicked harder.

Gabriel kept one eye on the duck-dinos the whole time. They'd clambered out on the other side and were slipping and sliding through the mud churned up by a herd of large hairy, horned creatures a little way up the bank.

The twins observed the behavior of the herd with fascination. The older creatures formed a loose protective circle around the young and the elderly while they drank from the river. The smallest of them played in the mud at the water's edge.

They had just about reached the halfway point the river when out of nowhere a massive scaled beast rose jaws-first out of the water, latched onto one of the hairy creatures, and dragged it under.

Alexis screamed.

John looked to see where the danger was coming from. Gabriel pointed at the ruckus on the riverbank, and John kicked to alter their course a little. They finally reached the bank, and the children scrambled onto solid ground while John waded through the shallows.

The mud pulled at their legs, and Alexis became mired until John stomped through and scooped her onto his shoulder.

Gabriel found a path of sorts. He hopped from one grassy tussock to another until the protrusions joined together and his feet landed without a squelch. He stood watching the carnage unfold farther upriver while he waited for John and Alexis. The hairy creature was being torn to pieces in the shallows by a number of the giant predators as the rest of the herd bellowed and stamped helplessly at the water's edge.

John reached dry ground and deposited Alexis beside her brother.

Alexis grabbed a handful of grass and tried to brush some of the mud off. "Next time, we build a bridge or go around or learn how to fly!"

Gabriel grinned. "That was a close one!"

Michael and Scott sat back on the couch, and Eric and Darryl relaxed. They had all been on the edge of their seats when the enormous reptile had attacked the pachyderm with the children so close by.

"Gabriel wasn't at all afraid," Darryl noted. "Kid's got balls already."

Michael smirked.

Scott let out a low whistle. "That was too close. Bethany Anne is going to kill you when she finds out they could have been eaten."

Michael shrugged, not taking his eyes from the screen. "Eve, what are the chances of the children dying?"

"Zero, Michael," she replied. "You don't want them to die at this stage."

Scott didn't try to hide his disbelief. He turned to Michael. "You're really going to let them die? I thought you were kidding about that."

Michael frowned. "I would never joke about something so serious as my children's lives."

Eric and Darryl looked between Michael and the screen with utter shock.

Scott gaped. *"Really?"*

Michael nodded. "Yes, really. Just not right now. They are not ready for that lesson yet."

Eyebrows went up at "yet."

"What about John?" Darryl asked.

Michael shrugged again and tuned out.

Eve sniffed. "Well, John owes me money from a bet he lost last week. Things are *very* iffy for him."

CHAPTER SIXTEEN

Independent Trading Vessel *Maiden's Rage*, Meeting Room

The captain of the *Maiden* slammed his fist on the table to silence the squabbling. "Quiet, all of you! We lost too much time on the last drop-off, not to mention the loss of profit because we were late on delivery."

The officers stared at the captain, muted by his show of violence. The first mate, Brakely, who had been with him for more years than Einoch could count, scrutinized him. "You okay, Einoch?"

Einoch waved to indicate he was. "It's just the time constraint on this load. We need to make it to the next drop-off before we forfeit the next payment as well." He straightened. "So I want your suggestions on how we cross this part of space without getting stopped by pirates or customs, not endless bitching about whose fault it was we were late."

"The ship has Gate tech," Brakely offered. "I wasn't

going to ask, but we've all been wondering why you haven't used it to get us out of this mess already."

The captain shook his head. "Gating into unknown space is fucking dangerous. I don't want to use the Gate drive unless it's an emergency."

"This *is* an emergency," Brakely argued. "We're going to be stuck out here in a dead ship if we don't get paid."

Einoch wasn't quite convinced. "That's another factor none of you are considering. With the size of the ship, it's just too expensive to Gate. Besides, we haven't had this ship long enough to have figured out the systems. We have no idea how to fix it if the drives fail. Every jump we take is a *risk*."

The crew didn't quite break out in an argument. However, Einoch could see from the looks that passed around the table that they were skating on the edge of mutiny. Nothing like a failed job or two to foment discontent in a crew who hadn't been through the shit together.

Einoch sighed. He missed piracy, where subordinates did as they were damn well told or faced the penalty of his wrath.

Of course, he hadn't liked facing the penalty himself, so here he was on a stolen Leath ship herding a crew of almost-legitimate traders.

Einoch gave his first mate a sour look. "Stow it, Brakely. If I'd wanted your opinion, I'd have thrown you a biscuit. Give me solutions."

The line of stumpy ganglia that ran front to back along the center of Brakely's skull rippled. "You have my recommendation, Captain. This is a Leath ship, and outside of Empire technology, you won't find anything stronger or sturdier. We can defend ourselves if necessary."

"Yeah," someone piped up from the far end of the table. "Fuck the expense. We'll more than recover the cost with this payday. That's if you pull your heads out of your asses and take the risk to gain the profit."

Einoch shrugged. He couldn't argue with that logic. He stood and placed his hands on the table. "Profit is the priority, right?" The faces of his officers showed him he'd made the right choice. "Well, what are you waiting for? Get us shipshape and ready to jump."

Brakely grinned. "That's more like it. Right, you heard the captain. I want every station and every area of the ship to sparkle. We're not going to jinx this by running dirty."

The crew hustled to it.

Devon, First City, Residential Area

Sabine ended the call to their ops manager and turned to the others. "Did you get all that?"

Ricole shook her head. "I did, but I don't understand. What did she mean by 'we'll get support info at a later date?'"

Jacqueline and Mark shared a gleeful glance. "It means we're here with no instructions until the infrastructure is put in," the Were told her.

Mark took over. "Until then, it's just the other six teams and us, and all we have to do is get settled and work our way into society here."

"And keep feeding the data back home," Jacqueline finished.

Sabine's face shone. "It is carte blanche, pretty much. Have any of you seen Demon today?" None of them had. She all but skipped out of the room. "I'm going to go call her. Devon is working out to be the *most* fun!"

Ricole was lost again. "What does 'carte blanche' mean?"

"Permission to do as we wish," Jacqueline explained. "In other words, we cannot cross the line because there *is* no line to cross."

"We have no rules?" Ricole scratched her cheek as she took that in.

Mark laughed. "It makes sense if we're going to blend in here."

Sabine returned to the room and started gathering her things to leave. "The question is what we're going to do with the time. We need to find jobs."

Mark rubbed his chin. "We have all the opportunity Michael afforded us. We just need to make the most of it. That means bringing this city in line with what Michael and Bethany Anne want for the planet as a whole."

Ricole considered this. "Correct me if I'm wrong, but isn't this place *supposed* to be a den of thieves and fucknuts?"

Jacqueline grinned. "Fucknuts?"

Ricole shrugged. "I heard Tim call Ricky that word in the APA, and it seemed appropriate. My point is, do we really want to work for some shady criminal just to pay the bills?"

Sabine sat down. "That's a good point. Why work for someone else when we have the wealth and skills between us to support ourselves?"

Mark pointed at her. "Exactly. So, suggestions?"

"We could open a trading company," Jacqueline suggested.

Ricole grinned. "Black market? I have some experience with that." She shrugged at the looks they gave her and inspected her claws. "What? I grew up on the *real* Devon. Did you think I got by on just my charm?"

Jacqueline chuckled. "Gray market should be deep enough for now. We just need to figure out the best way to set it up." She grabbed a notepad and pen and narrowed her eyes in thought. Mark grinned when the tip of her tongue appeared as she jotted her thoughts down. A couple of minutes later she looked back up. "Okay, this is what we need. One of us to lead, one for intelligence and communications, and two for muscle. Three to do the job, and two to run it."

Mark raised his hand. "I vote you for the lead."

Jacqueline shook her head. "Nuh-uh. I want to be muscle."

Ricole wasn't being left out. "Me too. I'm *all* muscle."

"What about me? I'm not staying behind while you two get all the action." Sabine glared at her fellow females, daring them to challenge her.

Jacqueline slammed the pad down and met Sabine's gaze with a slight growl, so Mark cut in before it degraded into something physical. "We can't *all* be muscle. We'll rotate through the roles so we all get a turn, how about that?" He raised his hands when they snapped their heads toward him. "That seems fair to me. I'll take intelligence first, so that frees up one spot."

Jacqueline shrugged and went back to taking notes. "I

guess I can take lead first, but next rotation I get to kick some ass."

They couldn't argue with that. Sabine backed down and began to pace with her hands behind her back. "Okay, so we rotate. Next, how are we going to run this company? We need a place to run it from, and...do we need to find employees?"

Jacqueline looked up from her pad. "What for?"

Sabine shrugged. "I don't know. Say we have a cargo that's too big to move quickly or a client who needs more protection than the five of us can offer?"

Demon strolled through the door, her tail swishing. *Who would need more protection than the five of us?*

"What the cat said," Ricole chipped in. "Besides, do we really want to involve unknowns? It could make maintaining our cover difficult."

Mark made a face. "Ricole is right. We would be better off automating as much of the heavy lifting as we can. Then we can operate without worrying that one of the workers will make us."

Sabine nodded, a sly smile forming. "We'll keep ourselves to ourselves, then."

Never let your prey see you approaching, Demon commented. She vaulted elegantly onto the window seat and tilted her face to the window to catch the sun. *I'm sure that applies here as well.*

Jacqueline picked up her pad again and started scribbling. "Right, Mark, you start searching for premises that we can keep bug-free. I'll get started on ordering what we need for setup, to be delivered from High Tortuga." She looked at Sabine, Ricole, and Demon. "You three get out into the city and start listening. We need to learn about this place, and how to take it over." She rummaged in a drawer and pulled out a small package. "This arrived while you were all still asleep this morning."

Ricole craned to see. "What is it?"

Jacqueline unwrapped the package and spread the contents out on the desk. "Our care package. We have a modified version of some of Tabitha's balls."

Mark snickered. "You said 'balls.'"

Jacqueline gave him a look that would have melted steel. "You and Tabitha both need to grow up."

Sabine snorted. "Are you going to tell Tabitha that to her face?"

"Fuck, no. I'm angry, not stupid." Jacqueline rolled her eyes and threw the package of spheres to her. "Just take them to the bazaar and activate them. They'll work their way through the city and acquire all the information we need to get ahead of the competition."

Ricole tilted her head. "And by 'acquire,' you mean steal?"

Jacqueline shrugged. "All's fair in business."

Demon lifted her head. *What are we supposed to do while the tiny machines are stealing for us?*

Sabine clapped delightedly. "We get to go and take the temperature of the city." Sabine grinned when Ricole looked at her blankly. "That means that we're going bar-hopping, Ricole. I told you this place was going to be fun."

Yollin Sector, QBBS *Meredith Reynolds*, Open Court

Gabrielle staggered toward the corridor under the

weight of all her bags. "We should have gotten a few more carts," she complained. "My hands are raw!"

Jean looked over the top of the large crate she was carrying. "Suck it up, buttercup. We're nearly out of here now."

The four ladies moved with the thinning crowd, heading out of the court. The moment the coast was clear, Bethany Anne grabbed Tabitha, who grabbed Jean and Gabrielle, and transferred the four of them and all their goodies to the Reynolds' residence.

Patricia was waiting for them when they arrived. She took one look at the overly laden women and shook her head fondly. "Come on in, my dears. You can put your bags and things in the side room to the left there." She pointed the door out as she made her way back into the house. "Your father is in the living room, Bethany Anne. I'll be in the kitchen fixing drinks for you all, and I'll join you shortly."

They dumped their bags and went into the living room. Lance put his book down and stood up from the couch to greet them. "How was shopping?"

Tabitha laughed. "There's not a pair of size sevens left to buy anywhere on the station."

"That's not true," Bethany Anne protested. "I didn't like those white shoes in the third store."

Tabitha tilted her head. "I stand corrected. That *one* pair you didn't like."

Patricia came in with a large, icy pitcher and six glasses on a tray. She put the tray on the table and sat in the wing-back chair beside Lance's recliner. "What didn't you like?"

Jean chuckled and reached for one of the glasses on the tray. "A pair of shoes."

Patricia put a hand to her forehead and pretended to faint. "I never thought I'd see the day when you met a pair of shoes you didn't like."

Bethany Anne made a face and sipped her drink. "So, Dad, are you going to tell me about this issue you're having or keep me in eternal suspense?"

Lance chuckled. He shifted in his chair to get comfortable and reached for a cigar that wasn't there. "Dammit. Oh, well." He shrugged and picked his drink up instead. "I had a visit from one of the Noel-ni delegates while I was at that conference."

"Conference?" Bethany Anne asked.

Lance shrugged. "I'd have to ask Meredith which one it was. There are so many of the damn things these days they all just blur together. Anyway, Reia, the Noel-ni delegate... she came to me in my position as head of the Federation and asked me to intervene in a situation involving missing ships." He held up a hand before Bethany Anne could interrupt. "Before you say a word, it's not the Leath, Bethany Anne."

Gabrielle and Patricia were polite enough to suppress their giggles. Bethany Anne narrowed her eyes at Tabitha and Jean, then sat back down. "So who do we like for it? You have someone looking into it, I presume."

Lance lifted a shoulder. "That's the rub. The politics on this are a complete pain in the ass. Reia also took the petition to the other leaders of the Federation, so I can't exactly have a black-ops team make a run on it."

Tabitha leaned back with a smirk and crossed her legs. "Well, you *could.*"

Gabrielle clapped her hands and turned to Lance. "You can't send any of your teams, but *we're* not one of your teams."

Lance looked at them skeptically. "And what if you get caught? That shit will blow straight back in my face."

Bethany Anne snorted. "Who exactly is going to catch one of *my* ships?"

CHAPTER SEVENTEEN

Independent Trading Vessel *Maiden's Rage*, Bridge

Einoch leaned over the console as he built a map of the secondary Noel-ni system they'd landed in, as was his standard practice whenever they hit an out-of-the-way system.

It passed the time while the engineering crew recharged the Gate drives, and he'd made a pretty penny over the years selling updates to places that were a little off the beaten path. The market for directions to these kinds of places *never* waned.

He reviewed the ship's reports as the bridge crew forwarded them to him, and he worked on the chart. A skeleton bridge crew worked in silence under Brakely's direction, and the atmosphere on the bridge was almost peaceful. It was as close to downtime as Einoch got.

The peace was shattered by a Gate proximity alert.

Einoch waved distractedly at Brakely, who gave the order. The unexpected Gate appeared on the viewscreen. "Who is it?"

Brakely leaned over the screen in front of him. "Looks like Noel-ni, five ships."

Einoch was doubly glad he'd had them stay well back from the system's core insert lines. "Are we secure?"

Brakely nodded. "I believe so, Captain."

Einoch nodded and returned to examining the scene beyond the hull of his ship. The light from the Gate flooded the space around it, making the five ships' progress easy to track. They cleared the Gate and changed course toward the planets in the distance. His eyes were drawn to a large, blank spot in the starry canvas some way away, between the ships and their destination. He pointed it out to the first mate. "What in the galaxy is *that?*"

Brakely had nothing.

Einoch turned back to the screen. "Are the Noel-ni aware they're heading straight for it? Track them, Brakely. Let's see what happens, but be careful not to reveal our position."

"I think they're going to miss it," Brakely told him a few minutes later. He turned to the captain with concern written all over his ganglia. "What the hell is big enough to block out the stars?"

Many of the bridge crew were on their feet, watching the clueless ships pass within kilometers of the dark behemoth.

"Oh, *fuck.*"

Einoch snapped his attention to the source of the curse. "What?"

"We have incoming, and they don't look too happy with us." The officer tapped at her console and pointed at the viewscreen. "They've picked up on our active sensors."

Einoch stared at the screen in alarm, seeing that some smaller ovoid object had broken away from the unidentified mass and was headed straight for them. "Get a boot up engineering's ass!" he yelled. He turned to Brakely, who was running from station to station. "How long have we got?"

Brakely wiped the sweat from his forehead. "Approximately two hours, Captain."

Einoch got on the comm. "All stations, you have two hours to get us the hell out of here."

The officer at the com tugged on Brakely's sleeve and pointed to her screen. Brakely looked down, and his ganglia went crazy. "Um... Einoch?"

Einoch's eyes widened at his first mate's lapse in protocol. "What is it, Brakely?"

"Make that an hour and a half. It just increased its speed."

Einoch thumbed the comm again. "Make that ninety minutes to get as much charge in this ship as possible." He put the ship on red alert.

"For all the good it'll do us..."

QBBS *Meredith Reynolds,* Queen's Private Dock

The stateroom was stuffed with the bags they had returned to drop off. Bethany Anne picked her way across to hug Lance before he left for dinner with Patricia and they left for home. "It's been so good to spend some time with you all, Dad."

Lance squeezed her extra tight. "We owe you a visit next time, okay?"

Bethany Anne was about to reply when Meredith pinged them. "What's up?"

Meredith's smooth voice came over the speaker. "There is a situation at All Guns Blazing. AGB security has requested aid, but I pulled the request in case you wanted to deal with it personally before returning to High Tortuga, my Queen."

Bethany Anne tilted her head and shrugged. "I'll bite. What have we got?"

Meredith chuckled dryly. "I thought you might. There is an all-out brawl in progress, and the bouncers are having trouble containing it."

Bethany Anne's mouth twitched. "Why not? It's not as if *Baba Yaga* left."

Tabitha danced around the bags on the floor and punched the air. "Whoo! Bar fight!" She stopped mid-jump and looked at Gabrielle with all seriousness she could muster. "You know they're my favorite, right?"

Jean grinned and excused herself, taking Gabrielle with her.

Bethany Anne turned to her father. "Love you, Dad."

Lance cupped her chin and kissed the top of her head. "Love you too, pumpkin. Now go and have some fun."

Jean and Gabrielle returned shortly after Lance had left, carrying a large crate between them.

"What's in the crate?" Bethany Anne asked as they placed it on the table.

Jean pressed her hand to the lock. It read her DNA and clicked open. "Come and see." She lifted the lid with a flourish and stood back while Bethany Anne examined the contents.

Bethany Anne pulled out the armored suit inside and held it up. "How do you always know what to get me?"

Jean grinned. "Not just you, all of us." She lifted the tray the armor had been on to reveal another suit on the tray below. She handed it to Gabrielle, then pulled out another for Tabitha, and finally one for herself.

They quickly changed into the suits, and Bethany Anne made the switch to Baba Yaga. She looked the others over and pursed her lips. Below the neck, she couldn't tell who was wearing the suits—male or female, human or just humanoid. However, three of the most famous faces in the galaxy looked back at her. "You're all going to have to hide your faces somehow."

Jean shook her head and pointed to a spot on her suit collar. "Just press here and your helmet will engage. Same again to retract it." She demonstrated, and the collar extended to form an opaque helmet. "HUD, as you'd expect."

Tabitha played with her helmet button. "Okay," she stated as she looked at her HUD. "This is pretty fucking cool, Jean. Nobody will have a clue they're getting their asses kicked by the FBB."

"I'm probably going to regret this, but what does FBB mean?" Jean asked.

Tabitha paused, her helmet still off. "Four badass bitches!"

Gabrielle coughed. "Um…that title is already taken. By the guys and me."

Baba Yaga narrowed her eyes for a second, then inspiration hit, and she cackled. "The Queen can have her Bitches, you three are now my Bastards."

"Talk about reverse gender discrimination," Tabitha muttered, but not loud enough to bug Bethany Anne's alter-ego.

Baba Yaga ignored her. "Meredith, are the AGB offices clear?"

"They are," came the reply.

She gave a sharp grin and held out her hands to the others. "Then what the hell are we waiting for?"

High Tortuga, Space Fleet Base, Immersive Recreation and Training Scenario, Dinosaur Island

The terrain had changed again in the hours since they'd left the river behind, the rolling grassland gradually morphing into a rough and rocky landscape that became increasingly difficult to navigate the closer they came to the long shadow of the mountain.

The land rose in jagged steps, which they had to climb to keep going toward the mountain.

Alexis kicked the rocky barrier. "This is ridiculous! *Why* can't we talk to Phyrro? He would have gotten us out of here an hour ago!"

John examined the rock face for the best place to climb up to the next level. "How effective is it to have the solution handed to you in training, Alexis?"

Alexis sniffed. "I suppose it isn't."

John cupped his hands to give the children a boost onto the ledge above. "'You suppose?' That's a little vague for a girl who loves precision."

She rolled her eyes and hopped onto his hand. "Okay,

you're right." She jumped for the ledge and pulled herself up.

Gabriel was next. He hauled himself over with ease and dusted himself off. He peered over the edge at John, who was backing up to take a running jump. "Dad could have given us at least *some* information," he grumped. "He saw how excited we were to play the game."

John landed on the mossy rock beside them. "Why would you expect that of him?" he asked. "Your father is wise, creative, and sneaky." He looked them each in the eye. "He is also completely dedicated to making sure you two get the upbringing you need to be able to handle the power you're gonna have when you grow up. You both know that, yet neither of you questioned why he'd let you play a game with no training value?"

Alexis made a sound of frustration. "Nuance! He even *told* me!" She stalked off, kicking the rocks as she went. "I can't believe we walked right into the very first trap he—*AHHHHH!*" She screamed as she disappeared from sight.

Gabriel started forward. "Alexis!"

High Tortuga, Space Fleet Base, Michael's Office, Vid-Doc Room

"Now *that* was ironic." Eve turned from the screen to see the stony reception her joke got from the guys. "No? She was bitching about Michael's trap, and she fell right into a trap." Michael fixed her with a stern look.

She shrugged and turned back to the screen. "Whatever."

189

John and Gabriel stood on the rim of the pit and searched the darkness below for any sign of Alexis.

"I can't *see*! Where is she?" Gabriel leaned over, and John pulled him back. "I'll jump in and pull her out," he told John.

"And what if you land on your sister?"

Gabriel made a face. "Then we need to find something to lower me down there." He looked around frantically, spotting a tall, vine-choked tree. "That tree wasn't there a minute ago."

John looked around. There weren't any other trees around, and Gabriel was right about that one appearing from nowhere. He shrugged. "Don't look a gift horse in the mouth, kiddo."

They ran over to the tree, and Gabriel pulled at a likely looking vine. It didn't budge an inch.

"Here, let me," John told him. He wrapped the vine around his forearm and gave it a sharp downward tug. The vine came away farther up the trunk, dislodging a shower of bugs and dead leaves. He shook them off and pulled again, and more of the vine came loose. He wound the vine around his arm as he walked around the tree and freed some more of it.

Gabriel heard a dry rustle in the leaves above them as John bent over to tear the vine from the ground. He glanced up in time to see a snake fall from the branch above John's head. "Uncle John!"

John managed to get an arm up before the snake latched onto his face. However, it sunk its fangs deep into his forearm. "*Fuuuu...*owww!" He tore the snake loose, twisted it around, and ripped its head off.

Gabriel eyed the fangs sticking out of John's arm warily. "You okay, Uncle John?"

John picked the fangs out and tossed them aside. "Sure, it only hurt for a minute. Now let's see about getting your sister out of that hole."

Eve chuckled and muttered, "Interest is a bitch, John."

Darryl and Scott exchanged worried glances.

Scott leaned over and whispered, "What did Eve and John get into that she's so pissed at him?"

Darryl shrugged and spoke just as low. "I have no clue, but remind me to ask John if he makes it out of there so I can avoid it."

CHAPTER EIGHTEEN

QBBS *Meredith Reynolds*, All Guns Blazing Offices

Baba Yaga gave Tabitha a little shove to move her from the Etheric to the office. Tabitha stepped into the office, and the roar of the brawl was obvious. She grinned in anticipation and waited a beat for the others.

Jean, Gabrielle, and Baba Yaga appeared within a few seconds, accompanied by a loud thump and then a crash as someone hit the office door from the other side.

Gabrielle chuckled as she made for the door. "Oh, goody, it's a big one!" Her voice sounded gravelly through the helmet's voice modulator.

"That's what *she* said," Tabitha snarked, pushing past to her get to the door first. "And it's first come, first served, so I'm leading." She yanked the door open and looked down the corridor to the main bar area, where the chaos was even more complete. Furniture flew, the crashes punctuating the overall soundtrack of yelling, roars, and breaking glass. "Shiiit," She looked back at her friends. "This is a full-on blowout."

Baba Yaga came to stand beside her and sniffed. "You're right. We can't break it up just yet, not with this many frustrated Wechselbalg involved." She pressed her lips together and assessed the severity of the fight. "Hmmm…"

"What are you thinking?" Jean asked.

Baba Yaga tilted her head. "That nobody here is trying to kill anyone, they're just blowing off steam. I have a mind to let it run its course for now."

Gabrielle's shoulders dropped. "No fight for us?"

Baba Yaga snickered. "Oh, we're *going* to fight. We'll help the bouncers make sure it doesn't go too far, and after it's done, I have the perfect place for all those frustrated Wechselbalg."

"Where?" Tabitha looked at her, then laughed. "You're shitting me. *Devon?*"

Baba Yaga nodded. "You know it."

The corridor heaved with angry bodies doing their best to pound the shit out of each other.

Tabitha saw a human standing over another human with his foot raised. The guy on the floor definitely didn't need a kick to the ribs, so Tabitha decided it was as good a place to start as any and punched the standing guy in the face. "Not so fun when they can fight back, huh?" She snickered as he crumpled to the floor.

She stepped over him and looked back at the others. "You three just going to stand there?"

Baba Yaga was by her side in a blink, and the four worked their way through to the main bar area in a storm of kicks, punches, and judiciously applied elbows.

High Tortuga, Space Fleet Base, Michael's Office, Vid-Doc Room

Addix pushed the plastic curtain aside and followed Eve's directions to the Vid-doc room. The screen wall caught her eye as she entered, distracting her from her purpose. Bethany Anne and Michael's children were playing some VR game with John, while Michael and the rest of the guys watched from the seating area and Eve puttered around the room.

Michael gestured for Addix to join them, and she took a seat and a handful of popcorn from the bowl Eric held out.

She munched a few pieces, her mandibles twitching with joy as Alexis had one of her little willful moments on the screen.

She waved her fists and kicked the loose rocks as she voiced her displeasure with her father. Addix thought it utterly endearing that so much force of will could be contained in such a sweet little creature.

Suddenly, Alexis screamed and was gone from the screen.

"Where did she go?" Addix asked Michael.

"There's a trap," he replied. "This part of the game is littered with them. Gabriel will have to work to get her out, with John's help."

Her mandibles conveyed her concern for Alexis.

Scott elbowed Darryl. "Aunt Addix is on the case now. She's not going to want to see the twins hurt."

Addix turned to Michael. "Is this true? They can be hurt in this game?"

He nodded. "This is not a game. They are in training."

"You are ensuring that they suffer?" Her mandibles picked up speed, and her translation software struggled to keep up. "Of all the... Wait until Bethany Anne hears about this!"

Michael's eyes flared red, and he put up a hand to silence Addix. "Enough. I respect your love and your effort, Addix, but my children are...*my children*. You will see that they are learning from this." His face softened a touch. "The longest-remembered lessons are the hardest and most painful to learn; you know that."

Addix looked at the screen, where Gabriel was working with John to retrieve Alexis from the pit. "Hmmm. Very well." She turned to Michael, still agitated. "I came to see you because the issue of Lance's we spoke about has intensified somewhat. The Noel-ni have lost more ships, and the Federation has gotten involved."

"I see." Michael steepled his hands under his chin for a moment, taking the news in. "Do they know what's causing the ships to vanish? What measures is Lance having the Federation take?"

"The system has been quarantined until the reason can be ascertained. The Noel-ni have no clue what the cause of the disappearing ships is. It could be anything from pirates to space monsters."

"It could also be Kurtherians," Michael noted.

"It could." They continued watching the children while Addix gave him a brief outline of everything she'd learned from her Federation contacts. "Unfortunately, the political situation is rather tenuous. The original vanished ships were fulfilling a trade obligation, and there is a real chance that war could break out between the Noel-ni and the other side unless the consignment—or at least proof of its destruction by a third party—is presented."

Her mandibles continued to broadcast her agitation. "That is not my only concern, Michael. When is Bethany Anne due to return to High Tortuga?"

Michael smirked. "You are thinking along the same lines as me, then?"

Addix' mandibles twitched in amusement. "I suspect she's already on her way to the quarantined system."

Michael sighed. "That's about what I was thinking." He got up and walked over to the console. "CEREBRO, get me a line to the Security Pit."

"Right away, Michael," the EI replied.

Jennifer came on the line a second later. "What can I do for you, Sir?"

"This is not a drill. Ready the fleet." He had to work to keep the grin out of his voice as he spoke. He'd been waiting for the opportunity since the base had been in the inception phase.

"The fleet, sir?" Jennifer recovered quickly. "Of course. What are their instructions?"

Michael paced in front of the console. "Tell them to warm up and be ready to leave within twelve hours. If we need to go sooner, we'll warn them we're going to prepare for a three-hour lift off."

"What's going on?" Eric asked.

"My wife," Michael stated, "won't leave well enough alone. I'm just making sure we have the firepower to back her up against whatever is out there. She would jump into Hell with a box of matches and a package of firecrackers. It isn't the wisest choice, so we will consider this an unplanned test of the fleet's readiness."

QBBS *Meredith Reynolds*, All Guns Blazing

Baba Yaga held two snarling wolves up in front of her by the scruffs of their necks. They twisted and clawed to escape her iron grip, which just made her hold on all the tighter. "Enough!" She banged their heads together to knock them out and dropped them, moving on to the next situation without a pause. She'd let the staff know she was there and that she would be responsible for damages, then threw herself into the fray with abandon.

It was satisfying to fight for no other reason than the sheer joy of it.

To pit herself against someone not because they were threatening the ones she loved, but simply because they challenged her to bring the pain or take it.

Jean and Gabrielle were dealing with a knot of drunken Wechselbalg in one corner of the bar.

Jean, keeping it minimal as always, laid the ringleader out with a headbutt.

Tabitha dashed past after a Shrillexian, who she was laying into with the pool cues she had acquired. The Shrillexian beat a hasty retreat for the exit before Tabitha could continue the lesson in fairness. She used the sticks to point behind her. "Asshole was picking on those little furry guys back there."

Bethany Anne looked over to where Tabitha had jerked her pool cue before running off to check on them. The "little furry guys" had teeth as sharp as her own, and they didn't seem to mind using them in the least.

She rolled her eyes and stepped over an unconscious Yollin to go and help Tabitha dislodge them from her legs.

The brawl was showing no sign of slowing, since word had spread that the bar fight to end all bar fights was going on. There was a long line of people waiting outside to keep the numbers steady. It was getting late, however, and they had an honest-to-fuck mission the next day.

Wrap it up, ladies, she told Gabrielle and Jean. She used her foot to scrape the small furry beings from Tabitha's legs and jumped onto one of the few remaining tables. She kicked away the wolf who tried for her legs and pressed the button on her helmet.

"Enough!"

The bar was plunged into silence when the figure on the table removed her helmet and revealed herself to be Baba Yaga.

Sam and Lucas shared a terrified glance.

"We're in the shit now!" Sam whispered shakily.

His brother sucked in short, rapid breaths. "The She-Witch was fighting... Shit, with us *all*."

Sam hadn't considered that, and he was nowhere near as afraid of her as his brother was. Personally, he found the scary look pretty damn—

"Why is she looking at you, bro?"

Sam swallowed, his face going red.

Baba Yaga grinned dangerously and addressed the bar. "Fight's over, everyone. Make sure you pick up your belongings and your unconscious friends on your way out."

It was more than disconcerting to hear the cheerful thanks given in that grating voice. When Baba Yaga spoke, her voice tripped every nerve in Lucas' and Sam's young Wechselbalg bodies. The instinct they felt most clearly was the one to flee.

Not everyone could move. Some stayed rooted to the spot, transfixed like animals in headlights.

Baba Yaga saw their reactions. She clapped her hands, and two energy balls appeared over her palms. "Anyone still present in two minutes time is going to be hot-footing it out of here."

Their feet suddenly unstuck.

High Tortuga, Space Fleet Base, Immersive Recreation and Training Scenario, Dinosaur Island

John and Gabriel descended into the darkness, held securely by the vine. The pit was less deep than they'd originally thought. The light was blocked by the twists in the drop, which hid the bottom from anyone looking down from above.

Gabriel began to search for his sister the moment his feet touched the ground. He was drawn to a glow up ahead. The light came from a pool at the bottom of a steep decline. He saw a spot of what looked to be blood in the light cast by the pool.

"Alexis!" He rushed forward, and almost fell over a jagged crack in the floor.

John grabbed Gabriel's arm to stop him from falling into the glowing liquid. "Easy, now."

Gabriel peered into the pool and made out a vaguely human shape in the glowing gloop below. He pointed and stared at John impatiently. "But she's down there, and she could be hurt!"

John joined Gabriel at the edge and identified the shape as Alexis. "So she is. Hang on a minute." He hopped in, slid down into the gloop, and scooped Alexis out. She spluttered and drew a breath, but didn't regain consciousness.

Gabriel hopped from foot to foot as John cradled Alexis in one arm and climbed back out. John gently laid her on the ground and turned her on her side.

Gabriel ran over and touched her sleeping face. "Is she okay?"

I'm fine, she answered groggily in their minds. She coughed weakly. *Or at least I would be if Dad and Eve hadn't put this stuff down here to knock me out! That's cheating!*

John wiped the rapidly-drying gloop from her face with his sleeve. "It could have been designed to kill you. Instead, you had an unscheduled nap and learned something. Want to tell me what that was?"

Alexis opened her eyes and rubbed them vigorously to clear the last flakes. "That no matter how many times I think I've figured out what my dad is up to, he's going to surprise me again? Okay," she admitted, huffing at John's serious expression. "I suppose that's true. If I'd been paying attention instead of griping, I would have seen the trap."

"I learned that you can tear the head off a snake," Gabriel told his sister. "It squelches."

Alexis paled. "Gross, Gabriel."

John shook his head and set off toward the next ledge.

High Tortuga, Space Fleet Base, Michael's Office, Vid-Doc Room

"I suppose that was a good lesson," Addix admitted.

Eve grinned. "I know. I designed it."

Michael glanced at the screen wall from his place at the console and smiled warmly at his children. Alexis and Gabriel were progressing through the trials even faster than he'd anticipated.

It was a good thing he'd listened to Eve about making it so the children experienced everything in real-time, since he needed the long High Tortuga night to go and make sure that they had a mother to return to when they emerged from the Vid-doc.

He reviewed the readiness reports as CEREBRO fed them from the ships to his station. Kael-ven's name was at the top of each report, so Michael opened a line to the Yollin.

"What can I do for you, Michael?" Kael-ven sounded hopeful. "You did get my reports? The fleet will be ready when you ask."

"Thank you, my friend."

"Don't thank me with words," Kael-ven grumped. "I've got the *G'laxix Sphaea* all dressed up, but there's nowhere to go, and you didn't even think to ask her to the dance, did you?" He chuckled, the clicks echoing over the comm.

Michael chuckled in return. "I think we both know who wants to be asked to dance, Kael-ven. Do you have a *full* crew?"

"You know he does," Kiel's voice cut in. "Just point us at whoever pissed Bethany Anne off, and we're good to go."

CHAPTER NINETEEN

QBBS *Meredith Reynolds*, General Reynolds' Office

Lance was at his desk the next morning when Meredith interrupted with an urgent request. "What is it, Meredith?"

"An independent trading ship, which we have traced as being a Leath freighter stolen from a pirate company, broke the quarantine on the system a little over an hour ago. The captain stood down immediately and requested a tight-beam link to you. They've complied with all our requests so far."

Lance frowned. "Interesting." He reached into the drawer on his right and grabbed a cigar. "Put the captain through. Let's see what they have to say before we blow them up."

Meredith opened the video link, and the terrified captain appeared. He held his hands up in supplication and jumped in before Lance could say a word. "Oh, thank the fucking *stars*! General, before you blow us to shit, you have to understand that we had no way of knowing we were jumping into a quarantined area. We were running for our lives!"

Lance leaned in a little. "Oh, yes?"

The captain nodded frantically. "We were fucked, General."

"Fucked isn't the word," came a voice from behind the trader captain. "The Gate engine just melted on us!"

The captain shrugged at Lance's expression. "I knew it was a possibility. We're lucky we didn't explode."

Lance blew out in sympathy. "Then you were lucky three times. What or who were you running from?"

The captain's eyes widened. "To be frank, I don't know. Our sensors couldn't identify it, and none of us have ever seen anything like it before." His eyes misted over as he relived the terror of the pursuit. "All I can describe is this gigantic mass with a rage-on for anything that passed it. We were tracking a bunch of Noel-ni ships that Gated into the system just after we did when the behemoth caught our sensors and sent a... a...*something* after us. Hold tight for a moment...I'm sending all our sensor data now. Maybe your tech can make sense of it."

Lance sent the data to Meredith to review when it arrived and looked at the captain. "What happened next?" he asked.

The captain grimaced. "We held onto our asses and hoped like hell that the Gate engine charged before it hit us."

QBS *ArchAngel II*

Bethany Anne pushed her plate away and answered the request for a mental link from Lance. *Hey, Dad. What's up?*

Lance sighed. *There's been a development in the situation that you need to know about. Have you ladies set off yet?*

We're just finishing breakfast. Why?

A trading vessel broke the quarantine. They were chased by an unknown entity that looks to be the cause of our missing Noel-ni ships, but neither Meredith nor I can make heads or tails of the scan data the captain sent.

She held up a hand to stall Jean, who noticed her raised eyebrow. *Send it over, Dad. I'll have ADAM and TOM go through it.*

She received the data a few seconds later. *Got it.*

Be careful out there, sweetheart.

Her laugh was light in his mind. *What do you think I'm going to do?*

Lance's reply was quiet. *What you always do, Bethany Anne.*

Not this time, Dad, she assured him. *Alexis and Gabriel are my first consideration. The only reason I would risk leaving them without a mother is to save their lives. You know that.*

I know, Lance told her gently. *All the same, watch yourself out there. There's something off about the whole thing, and it's got my hackles up.*

Okay, I promise we'll be careful. You just keep the traders in the quarantine area until I get there.

Will do. He closed the link, and Bethany Anne pushed her chair back. "That was Dad," she told the others.

"What was he contacting you for?" Tabitha asked.

She got up to leave. "He got some information about whatever it is we're facing on this mission."

Gabrielle put her coffee cup down. "What did he have to say?"

"Not too much yet," Bethany Anne admitted. "You three get ready to leave. I'm going to go through the data he sent and see if I can't figure out who the culprit is before we get there." She drained her glass of juice and grabbed an apple to take to her room with her.

She brought up her HUD and looked over the logs of the *Maiden's Rage* as she walked to her quarters, skipping the sensor data in favor of the bridge transcripts.

ADAM, can you get on that sensor data and turn it into something I can use?

>>I love the way you ask, as if you don't know I've done it already.<<

Bethany Anne smirked as she made her way to her bedroom. She kicked her shoes off, got onto the bed, and sat back against the pillows with her legs curled under her. *So tell me what you have. You too, TOM. I know you can't resist poking your nose in.*

>>The scans aren't conclusive.<<

They don't need to be, TOM told them. **I may already know who we are up against.**

Well, don't keep us in suspense. What do you know?

It's not so much knowledge as a memory.

Bethany Anne held a hand to her forehead and laughed aloud. *I expect nothing less than some vague, half-helpful recollection from you. After all, why change the habits of a lifetime? Just tell me what you've been able to work out and we'll go from there, okay?*

Such faith. If you must know, I remember the incident perfectly well. When I was just an acolyte, one of the pilots returned from a planet which had been destroyed by an AI. It became corrupted and tore the planet to shreds to gather the resources to keep growing. She managed to scan the AI and escape with her life and her ship intact, and the data she shared was eerily similar to what we have here.

Well...fuck.

>>You don't say. This could turn into a complete clusterfuck, Bethany Anne. If this is an AI and its only goal is to grow and defend itself, you can be sure that it won't go down easily.<<

I remember the scenarios from when we were figuring out what you were going to do, ADAM. It's some scary shit. She shook her head. *But we can't get caught up in what might be. Get with Michael. We're going to need a little more firepower than we have.*

>>I'm on it.<<

And TOM, study that sensor data. Learn whatever you can from it. We're not going into this unprepared.

High Tortuga, Space Fleet Base, Michael's Office, Vid-doc Room

ADAM finished the brief, and Michael sat back to take it in. "AI gone wrong? How do we defend against that?"

"You go back two hundred years and build your own super-awesome AI," ADAM replied glibly. The speaker rattled with his laughter. "Oh, wait, you did! Looks like we're all set, then. Just get the fleet to where Bethany Anne is. The AI is sure to defend itself, and she won't back down no matter how much she keeps telling everyone she will."

"She probably has every intention of doing so." Michael shrugged. "She just doesn't know *how* to back down. We will be there, don't worry. Addix already told me about the situation, although she knew nothing about any AI. I began preparing the fleet immediately after her arrival."

"Then I guess we'll see you there."

Michael signed off and looked around the room. His gaze alighted on Addix, who had stayed to keep watch over the children. "Aunt Addix," he began smoothly. She looked at him with her head tilted in question. Michael grinned and pointed at the screen. "How would you like to babysit for a while?"

Addix looked at Eve skeptically. "I can have my knives in there, right?"

Eve nodded. "Relax, Addix. I'm not mad at *you*. You can have your knives, and we'll have fun. And I can hear you, so if you want me to, I can change things on the fly." She snickered and went back to monitoring the game.

Addix clicked her mandibles happily. "Then I would be honored to babysit!" She'd shed her robes as soon as she'd gotten there, so climbing into the last empty Vid-doc was no issue for her. Once again, she was grateful for the small freedoms that came with the acceptance of family.

She closed her eyes, and when she opened them again, she was in a craggy landscape. The children were at rest in the shade with John standing guard close by.

Alexis spotted Addix first. She grabbed her brother's arm and jumped up and down in her excitement. "Gabriel, look! It's Aunt Addix!"

Gabriel's face lit up just like his sister's. He too began to bounce when he saw her. "Aunt Addix!"

The twins rushed her and scrambled up her legs to be scooped into her arms. She held them close. "And how are my little hunters?"

The twins didn't need to be asked twice. They launched into a rapid and babbling recounting of their adventure so far. Addix inclined her head toward John, who nodded back. "Bye, kids," he called. He waved and was gone from the game.

Addix turned her attention back to the children. "Who wants a ride up the mountain?"

* * *

Michael observed his children's reaction to their Ixtali aunt. "Who would have expected them to bond so closely with Addix?" he mused.

"How humanocentric," Eve stated. "It makes perfect sense, actually."

Michael walked over to the Vid-docs. "How so, Eve?"

Eve didn't look up from her station. "Well, Addix loves them unconditionally. It's only natural that they would respond to that. Plus, she pampers them shamelessly. Look at her—she's already indulging them."

She pointed at the screen for emphasis, where Addix was climbing with the children perched on her back.

Michael inclined his head. "I suppose you're right. After all, they have been raised among many species. A couple of extra legs shouldn't be too off-putting to them."

Eve shrugged. "I don't see the issue with the Ixtali having four legs. Lots of species do."

Michael considered that. "Most of those species are mammalian or reptilian in appearance. The Ixtali have that whole hairy-legged spider thing going on. It takes some time to convince your brain not to run when you first meet them."

Eve raised an eyebrow. "And now?"

He grinned. "I didn't say *I* had that problem. I have admired and appreciated Addix and her dedication to my family from the start." His voice dropped slightly. "I would not allow her near the children if I did not trust her. The same goes for you, Eve. I trust the two of you to look after them for me while I am away."

"Of course we will," Eve assured him. "And we'll have fun, too."

"That's good to hear." Michael laid a hand on each of the children's pods. "Rest well, learn well, and be strong, my children. I will bring your mother back to you."

Eve heard him as he walked out. *"That is a promise."*

CHAPTER TWENTY

QBBS *Meredith Reynolds*, Large Meeting Room

The tiered seats were filled with gesticulating holograms.

The barrage of catcalls and angry shouting from the assembled Federation leaders echoing around the room for the last two hours had given Lance a headache.

He leaned on the lectern and rubbed his forehead, not caring if everyone in the room saw his frustration.

The screen at the back of the stage where he stood to chair the meeting was paused at the end of the footage from the indie trader vessel.

The Noel-ni leader had begun the meeting by admitting to the assembly that the Noel-ni had gone behind the Federation's back to negotiate a favorable trade deal with a non-Federation planet, which was now threatening war unless the deal was honored to their satisfaction.

The leaders had skipped completely past the loss of life

and impending war and zeroed in on what they'd missed out on with the underhanded trade deal.

None of them were focused on the larger issue.

Lance rolled his eyes at the squabbling leaders and addressed Meredith. *You would think that the emergence of a new and potentially extremely aggressive enemy would get them to pull their heads out of their asses and agree for one minute, but no. They want to continue the pissing contest. I'd be on my last nerve if it weren't for the fact that this circus is exactly what we need right now.*

I find it difficult to understand why the leaders do not make the most of the system set up for their benefit. Meredith sniffed. *However, that would require looking beyond simple self-interest. I suspect that to be a step beyond what most of the planetary leaders are capable of. It's too much like logical behavior.*

Lance sighed mentally. *Unfortunately, you're right. Then again, I knew heading the Federation was going to be more like herding battlecats at first than the meeting of minds we want to achieve. Politics is a game, and games attract children, Meredith.*

True, Meredith concurred.

It is what it is, and like I said, it works in our favor this time. Bethany Anne needs them distracted, so that's exactly what I'm going to do. Of course, I will not get noticed for what is going to be an Academy Award-level effort.

Lance straightened up to address the other leaders, who had been too busy arguing to notice he'd taken a step back from the debate. The Zhyn and Leath leaders had teamed up against the Noel-ni, who was defending himself from their vicious tirade with his own stream of abuse.

The holograms threw their arms around as they screamed at each other.

"Enough!" Lance barked. "I've had it up to here with all the bickering, backstabbing, and bullshit you all pull when you think nobody is looking. This is a *federation*, dammit! Start acting like allies, or I'll decide that my daughter is the best person to keep you all in line after all. All it will take is one call, and we'll be an Empire again."

The threat had the desired effect. Lance snickered internally at the effectiveness of what he was starting to see as his own particular version of, "Quit arguing, or so help me, I'll turn this car around."

"What exactly do you want us to do for the Noel-ni?" the Leath leader growled into the nervous silence. He pointed at Reia accusingly. "They got themselves into this mess by sneaking around to gain an advantage over the rest of us. Let them get themselves out of it as a *penalty*."

Lance noted how each of the leaders reacted to the Leath's statement. He raised an implacable eyebrow. "By that logic, the next time the Leath need assistance, the Federation should refuse on the grounds that you can get yourselves out of it. Still want to be an asshole about fulfilling your obligations? Go ahead."

The Leath leader looked around for support but found none. Lance's comment had hit home with the others. Even the Noel-ni leader fell silent.

"That's what I thought." Lance rolled his eyes and moved on. "Now, if you're all done debating who owes who what, we can get on with identifying a way to deal with this threat. We have no solid information yet, and we need to work toward changing that before the situation escalates further."

The Noel-ni leader raised a paw toward the screen on

the stage. "You all saw the video. Don't imagine that you are safe from this thing if we can't contain it."

Lance nodded in agreement. "We're going to send some advanced spy satellites out there. The ships we have out there right now don't have sophisticated-enough equipment. They will take around four days to reach the quarantined system, since we're not going to send them in from anywhere that will lead the enemy back to us. Once we have that data, we can decide where to go from there."

A flicker passed over the holograms as the leaders broke into debate once again.

I've passed all of this on to ADAM. Meredith snickered in Lance's mind. *I think you just bought Bethany Anne a little extra time.*

That was the plan, Lance told her.

High Tortuga, Space Fleet Base, QBS *G'laxix Sphaea*

"Good of you to give us a ride, Kael-ven." Michael slapped the captain on his arm as he passed him at the top of the ramp.

He waved back at John, Scott, Eric, and Darryl, who stood at the bottom of the ramp with all their ops gear stacked on antigrav carts. "I hope all this won't get in your way."

"You won't be in my way. Eve warned me you were loaded for leviathans, so I assigned you guys to the ship's APA while we're active and it's not in use. You'll have everything you need there."

Kael-ven stood back with a flourish as John and Scott

reached the top of the ramp with the first cart. "Welcome aboard."

John nodded. "Good to be here, Kael."

Michael adjusted his go-bag on his shoulder and waited for Eric and Darryl to maneuver the other cart up the ramp.

"A little overloaded there," Kael-ven commented as he and Michael walked down the corridor behind the others.

Michael shrugged as they came to a stop at the elevators. "I'd rather be overprepared than left with my ass hanging in the wind."

The Yollin's shoulders shook with silent laughter. "I honestly can't see you in that situation."

John turned around and grinned. "Pretty sure Akio could tell you differently, Kael."

Michael gave him a look that could crack permacrete.

"What?" John shrugged. "Akio talks to Tabitha, Tabitha talks to Peter, and Peter talks to us. It's kinda how we keep abreast of shit around here." The elevator doors opened and they all piled in except Kael-ven, who excused himself to return to the preparations. "It's rather efficient."

They left the elevator and made their way into the training room.

The guys immediately began unpacking the carts. Darryl went over the checklist as Eric and Scott got each one open.

Scott whistled. "We're going with heavy armor? That shit is just flat out sexy." He held up one of the flat black pieces to inspect it. "Jean just gets better and better at this."

"What's in the crates?" Eric cracked one of them open and pulled out a gleaming rifle from within. "Ohhh," he breathed. "John, we have to get Jean a thank-you gift when we get back. Have you seen this? She's spoiling us!"

"That's my Jean. She looks after her boys." John chuckled as he fixed the mini-missile launchers to Scott's shoulder plates. "Love the gift idea. I'll even help you pick something out."

Michael took his bag over to a weight bench and removed the smallish box he'd found waiting for him when he'd gone to retrieve his armor earlier. There had been nothing to indicate what was in the box or how to open it, which he hadn't been able to do.

"What have you got there?" Eric called.

Michael held the box up, and the smooth wood caught the light. "I'm not sure yet. A gift from Bethany Anne, I assume."

John nodded at the box. "Jean's proud of those. Have you figured out how to open it yet?"

Michael shook his head and ran a finger along the side. "I can't even find the seal." He glanced at John, who looked a little too nonchalant for his comfort. "You know how to open it?"

John held his hands palms up and shrugged. "Who, me? Maybe. All that time in the jungle must have clouded my memory."

Michael narrowed his eyes and stowed the box in his bag again. "Fine, don't tell me."

"Bethany Anne says that you'll work it out," ADAM cut in.

"She's listening?" Michael asked.

"She's got me listening in and giving her a running commentary," ADAM replied. "She says to tell you the ships are going to war, and to hurry your ass up. She doesn't want to start without you."

Michael grinned. "Tell her that if she does there will be hell to pay when I get there."

Eric had his leg up on a rack to fasten his armor. "Hey, if you're done flirting with your wife, the ship's taken off. We should get ready."

Michael chuckled and picked up his chest plate. "You have *met* my wife?" He shook his head. "I'll *never* be done flirting."

High Tortuga, Space Fleet Base, Immersive Recreation and Training Scenario, Dinosaur Island

Addix came to a stop on a wide plateau halfway up the mountain that had an opening into a cave. The children climbed down from her back and stretched their muscles after the long ride.

Alexis peered at the narrow opening in the rock, wary of traps after her earlier mishap. "Aunt Addix, what's in here?"

Addix stuck her head in to check. The cave beyond was cool and empty. "Nothing, Alexis." She looked up at the rapidly darkening sky. "We should camp here for the night. You two need some sleep."

"We don't have any camping equipment," Gabriel pointed out.

Addix' mandibles worked for a moment. "Well, I suppose I should have you both use the resources around you to create comfort."

Alexis yawned and rubbed her eyes. "Come on, Gabriel. You get the firewood, I'll gather soft plants for bedding."

Gabriel jumped to it.

Addix held up a hand to stall them. "I said I *should*. I didn't say I was going to." She laughed at the hopeful expressions on their little faces. "Eve?"

There was a flash of lightning, and a giant Eve appeared above them as if in a vision. The sky around Eve crackled with lightning, each flash adding to the soft golden glow of the nimbus surrounding her. Her wings held her aloft without beating, yet the wind from them rippled through her long dark hair and set the sweeping folds of her kimono dancing.

Alexis and Gabriel stared up at Eve, transfixed.

"How are you doing that?" Alexis yelled over the noise.

"God Mode, that's how," Gabriel breathed.

Addix waved at the android. "Nice outfit. Can we get some camping gear down here?"

Eve cut the light show and floated down to them, decreasing in size as she descended. She was her regular height when she landed. She came over to them, studying the plateau as she walked.

Addix nodded toward the cave. Eve waved a hand at the narrow aperture, and it was transformed. The dark opening was gone, replaced by a cheerful, cozy den. The entrance glowed invitingly, and a delicious smell came from the food waiting inside for them.

"I suppose a little luxury won't do them any harm," she told Addix with a wink.

"I won't tell if you don't," Addix replied with a chuckle.

"Thank you, Aunt Eve," the twins chorused.

Eve smiled. "You are very welcome, my angels. Now go and eat and rest well. When you wake up, you'll finish this scenario."

Gabriel pouted. "Oh, I don't want to stop playing!"

Alexis nodded her agreement. "Me either!"

"That's good," Eve told them, "since I have a new scenario ready and waiting for when you've crossed the mountain."

Alexis and Gabriel ran over and hugged Eve. "What's the new story, Aunt Eve?" Alexis asked.

"Well…" Eve hesitated for effect.

"Tell us, tell us!" Gabriel cried.

She grinned. "All I'm going to tell you is that it's based on a very old game from Earth. It has caves and dragons."

Alexis repeated the word with awe. "Dragons?"

Eve inclined her head. "Yes, but first you have to finish this scenario. The sooner you rest, the sooner you can complete it."

The twins hugged Eve again, then hugged Addix and ran for the den, chattering excitedly about dragons.

Eve turned to Addix. "Do you need to leave for a while to take care of your spy stuff?"

Addix shook her head. "No, I took care of anything time-sensitive before I entered the game."

Eve nodded and produced a tablet out of thin air with a flourish. "You can use this to check in on your messages if you need to. It has a button to hide it while you're not using it. Do you need anything else?"

"I'm good, thanks," Addix replied. She looked up from the tablet to see she was alone on the plateau. "Bye, then," she murmured.

She looked at the entrance to the den and smiled at the sound of the children's laughter. They had both done excellently in this scenario, and she had to admit that they had learned vital skills from the experience.

Still, *dragons?* Addix had studied Earth fiction—mostly so she could understand the references the humans constantly made—so she was aware of the nature of dragons. She couldn't help but wonder what Eve's new game was going to teach them.

CHAPTER TWENTY-ONE

Outside Quarantined System, QBS *ArchAngel II*, Viewing Platform

Bethany Anne rested her arms lightly against the railing as she looked into the expanse beyond. "It never ceases to make me stop and think."

Tabitha leaned against the railing beside her, lost in her thoughts. "What's that?" she asked distractedly, turning from the window to look at Bethany Anne.

"Space. The beauty of it all. The vastness." She shrugged at Tabitha's frown and returned to watching the streak in the distance that had set off this chain of thought. "Anything could happen out here. We're so small, and the potential for random destruction is so endless."

Tabitha tilted her head. "That's just a little morbid. We're about to go to war, and you're worried about some random comet? It's not like you to be distracted like this before a fight."

"I'm not distracted." Bethany Anne couldn't explain her

growing conviction that the universe wasn't as random as she'd been led to believe. How could it be? She'd lived long enough to figure out that life went in circles. Some circles were bigger than others, but at the heart of it, people were doomed to repeat the same mistakes over and over, no matter their species.

A prime example was her father's current political issues, which were markedly similar to the ones he'd faced back on Earth. While she had every faith in Lance's ability to pull the Federation kicking and screaming into something resembling the beacon of hope they'd intended, the petty dramas he was dealing with right now had no place in her larger vision.

However, she had to admit she'd been circling, just the same as everyone else.

Granted, it was a temporary diversion while she and Michael raised the children and readied themselves for the monumental ass-kicking they were preparing to deliver, but she still itched to get out there and complete her mission to create a galaxy where everyone could raise their children in peace and safety.

It was some distance from her original intent to storm the galaxy and rip the still-beating hearts from every Kurtherian she came across, but the overall *desire* was still the same.

Some women were softened by motherhood, but not Bethany Anne.

ArchAngel's voice interrupted them. "I have received a message to stand clear. The fleet is about to Gate in."

Gabrielle and Jean arrived on the viewing platform just as a Gate opened at a safe distance. It shimmered, lighting nearby space, and the fleet of High Tortuga came through. It was led by the *G'laxix Sphaea*, which slowed long enough for a single Pod to exit before continuing.

Tabitha looked out with wide eyes as the dreadnoughts flew in formation over the top of the *ArchAngel II*. She craned to see them, then turned to Bethany Anne. "Okay, I get what you mean. That made me feel like a minnow swimming around while the sharks go by."

"They're our sharks, Tabitha, and they're lining up ready to take a bite out of whatever the hell is out here." The Pod streaked toward them, and Bethany Anne let go of the railing. "That will be Michael and the guys. Time to start this dance."

They reached the docking bay as the Pod came through the translucent barrier. Michael was last down the ramp, waving at Bethany Anne and continuing to the meeting room.

"How are the children?" she asked him immediately.

Michael smirked. "Missed you too, my love." He caught her in his arms and kissed her. "The children are fine. Addix and Eve are taking good care of them."

Bethany Anne frowned. "Addix is babysitting?"

Michael nodded. "She volunteered. The children were so happy to see her that they didn't even miss John leaving."

They walked from the shuttle bay together, heading for the meeting room. "What have you had them learning while I've been away?"

Michael grinned. "Mostly problem-solving. They've blasted through the lessons, as always."

Bethany Anne nudged him with her shoulder. "Maybe

you weren't giving them enough credit when you designed the lesson."

Michael smirked. "Oh, the tasks are definitely challenging enough. Eve and I made sure of it. I got your gift, by the way."

"Have you worked out how to open it yet?" Bethany Anne chuckled when he shook his head. "I told Jean to make it a challenge since you don't like anything that comes easily. You're going to like what's inside, so don't take too long to figure it out."

Everyone was waiting when Bethany Anne and Michael entered the meeting room. Kael-ven gestured to the only empty chairs at the table. "Great, you're here."

Bethany Anne waved him off and pulled out one of the two chairs between John and Gabrielle. "I'm glad to see you, but we haven't got time for the niceties, Kael. Let's just get started with the briefing." Nods of agreement went around the table.

"The goal," she began, "is to come in from a separate direction than the Federation. Dad has made sure we have a little time before the Federation arrives. We will make an effort to communicate, and look for any Kurtherian influence."

"What if there is?" Gabrielle asked.

Bethany Anne allowed a cold smile to touch her lips. "If there is, we grab the information and then do what needs to be done. We will keep one ship far enough away to catch the data and Gate out if it goes to shit and they overwhelm us."

Kael-ven nodded to Kiel, who brought up a video on the wallscreen. "This is ADAM's enhanced version of the video from the trader vessel that broke the quarantine, for those who haven't seen it."

Bethany Anne saw a lot more detail than she had when viewing the original. "It looks like a big fucking rock. We're being attacked by a rock?"

"No," Kael-ven told her. "Keep watching the center quadrant."

The place he'd pointed out suddenly wavered and the rock vanished as a dark sphere came streaking toward the camera. Bethany Anne caught a glimpse of the massed shipwrecks beneath the illusion.

"Kiel, freeze it there." Bethany Anne stood and leaned in to get an even closer look. "Shit, that's some of the best cloaking tech I've ever seen."

TOM piped up over the speaker, "Possessing that technology would increase our likelihood of success in the long term."

His voice was replaced by ADAM's. "Maybe the species will be open to negotiating a price for it? If they aren't the homicidal assholes we're expecting, that is."

"There's a novel thought." Bethany Anne glanced at Michael, who was tapping a pen on the table as he scrutinized the window into the alien ship's true appearance. "So, we have a bunch of dead ships disguised as a rock. I guess that casts doubt on your AI theory, TOM."

"Not necessarily," he contended through the speakers. "There's an odd order to that mess of ships. If that construction is not the work of a logical mind come undone, I'll eat my hat."

Tabitha snorted. "You don't *have* a hat, TOM."

"It's a metaphorical hat, like everything else in my life," he grumped.

Bethany Anne rolled her eyes. "Focus, everyone. We need a plan of action."

"What's wrong with our usual plan?" John asked. "It's simple, and it's never failed us yet."

Bethany Anne tilted her head. "You mean, kick the doors in and kill everything in sight until there's nobody left to threaten the Federation?"

John nodded sagely. "That's the one."

High Tortuga, Space Fleet Base, Immersive Recreation and Training Scenario, Dinosaur Island

The children clung tightly to Addix as she looked up to check their progress. The peak was just ahead—if you could count scaling a fifty-foot perpendicular rockface as being "ahead."

They'd made most of the day's climb by themselves, but Addix had noticed them flagging as the sun began to drop and insisted they ride on her back again. When they'd reached the sheer cliff that was the final obstacle between them and the game's end task, she'd secured them to her. Now they were almost at their destination.

"Aunt Addix, do you know what the final challenge is?" Alexis asked.

Addix did know, but she had been instructed by Michael to give nothing away. "I do not," she told Alexis.

Alexis giggled. "Aunt Addix, I know you're lying. Your mandibles gave it away."

"They most certainly did not," Addix disputed. "I have

full control of my expression, thank you very much." She pulled with her hands and pushed with all four feet to haul them over the top of the cliff.

"Actually, that's what gave you away," Alexis told her sweetly. She and Gabriel undid their restraints and tumbled to the ground. The sun still gave plenty of light this high up, and the wind whistled as it whipped around the rocks. The peak rose in jagged spires around them; the only flat ground was where Addix had put them down.

"This place is a lot bigger than it looked from the bottom," Gabriel remarked. He started forward to explore the fissure closest to them, but Alexis pulled him back.

"It might be a trap," she cautioned. She turned to Addix. "Are you at least allowed to tell us what the task is?"

Addix nodded. "Yes, but as soon as I do the task will begin."

Alexis screwed her nose up in thought. "Okay. Is there anything else we should know about before we start?"

Addix chuckled. "Shrewd, Alexis. All I can tell you is to run swiftly, choose your path carefully, and trust yourselves."

"Is that all?" Alexis pouted. "Thank you and everything, but I don't think vagueness counts as actual advice, Aunt Addix. What is the task parameter?"

Addix pointed at the rocky spires. "The portal to the next scenario is at the center of the maze. All you have to do is reach it and activate it to complete this story. You must do this alone, but I will be waiting on the other side of the portal for you."

Alexis frowned. "We just have to find the portal and go through it? Where's the challenge?"

A sudden screech filled the sky. The twins looked up when a massive shadow blocked out the sun.

"Pterosaurs!" Gabriel cried.

"Run, children," Addix cautioned. "I will see you both very soon."

Alexis grabbed Gabriel's hand, and they made a dash for the cover of the rocks. They slipped into a gap and pelted along the twisting passages until the screeching was well behind them.

They stopped at a fork in the path, unsure which way to take.

Alexis picked up a loose rock and scratched a rough arrow into the stone.

"What are you doing that for?" Gabriel asked.

"We'll mark every split in the path that we take. That way, if we get lost or turned around, we can get back on the right path."

They had to follow the arrows back a couple of times over the next hour when they hit dead ends. The maze seemed to be endless. They made turn after turn, and the sense of urgency passed after a while.

They had just found their way back to the path after hitting yet another dead end when a sudden screech filled the air.

A pterosaur landed on the rock above them and began swiping at them, its leathery wings outstretched. Alexis scrambled through a gap that led to another part of the maze and Gabriel crawled through behind her. They emerged under an overhang, which gave them a few minutes to think while the winged beast screeched and flapped impotently in its rage at losing them.

Alexis tucked her arms around her knees and rested her head on them while she caught her breath. She looked up when Gabriel shook her arm. "Alexis, the portal!"

They had found the center of the maze.

The rock had been excavated to make a wide, clear space. A dais was in the center, surrounded by rows of carved stone benches. The portal was on the dais, a huge stone circle with symbols carved into every inch that Alexis and Gabriel could see.

Another screech cut the air as they dashed through the benches to climb the steps.

The pterosaur came to roost on top of the portal, blocking Alexis and Gabriel's exit from the game. They scrambled underneath one of the benches and huddled together.

Alexis peered at the beast, which was tearing chunks off the top of the portal and flinging them in its frustration. "How are we going to get past that thing?"

"I don't know," Gabriel answered in a soft, shaky voice. "Alexis…"

Alexis glanced in alarm at her brother's pale skin and clammy hands. "Gabriel? Are you okay?"

Gabriel looked at her with unfocused eyes. "Don't…feel sho goo…" He slumped to the side.

"Gabriel!" Alexis scooted over to him and cradled his head in her lap. "What's happened?"

On the other side of the portal, Addix watched Gabriel

slump to the ground on her tablet screen. "Was the arachnid necessary?" she asked Eve.

Eve shrugged. "They needed a nudge, and you are frankly rather inspiring."

"I should go in and make sure Gabriel is okay."

Eve shook her head at the agitation Addix was showing. "Don't worry, he's just asleep."

"You *ass*! You bit Gabriel!" Alexis yelled, crushing the spider with a rock before it could bite her brother again. "*Now* what am I going to do?"

She put her ear to Gabriel's chest. His heart beat slowly but steadily. "Aunt Addix! Aunt Eve! Gabriel is hurt!"

Neither of her aunts answered.

Alexis knew in that instant that this was a part of the game. She looked at the portal, her only hope of getting Gabriel out of here.

"Okay then, I'll defeat the pterosaur all by myself."

She made sure Gabriel was safe and crawled out from underneath the bench. The pterosaur lowered its head and bellowed at her, scratching at the portal as it beat its wings.

So it doesn't leave the portal. I wonder if it will change when I get closer? Alexis bared her teeth at the dinosaur and took a step forward. "You have one chance to let me take my brother through that portal," she yelled. Her mind worked the whole time furiously. *How do I get it to leave? Do I have to kill it? What would Mommy do?*

Alexis laughed aloud. She'd seen the videos of her

parents kicking ass and taking names. Since this was a virtual reality, could she do the same?

Gabriel moaned, dragging her from the rabbit hole she'd almost fallen into. "Daddy and his traps again!" He knew she was susceptible to the beauty of pure thought. She snapped her attention back just as the pterosaur began to beat its wings in preparation for taking flight.

Mommy wouldn't let anything stop her from saving someone, and neither would Alexis. She held up her hand just like she'd seen her mother do and willed the energy to come.

Nothing happened. "Hmmm..." Alexis knew that the energy came from the Etheric, but there was no Etheric here. Maybe there was some equivalent?

"How did Eve make the lightning?" she pondered.

She felt a tingle in her palm.

Addix laughed aloud. "Did you just give her the ability to make energy balls?"

Eve snickered. "She deserves it, just for having the courage to stand up to that thing armed with nothing but her temper. She's going to get her first taste of battle. I'm such a proud aunt."

A smug smile spread across Alexis' face as the energy ball formed in her hand. She flung it at the pterosaur, scoring a hit on its beaky face. "Get away from the portal!" she yelled.

The pterosaur screamed its pain and launched at Alexis from the top of the portal. Alexis screamed in return and threw two more energy balls at it, singeing its wings.

It wasn't enough.

Alexis thought on her feet as the pterosaur made an ungainly landing and came at her. She drew the energy, but let it build while she coaxed the beast away from Gabriel.

She led it step by step toward the opposite side of the dais, dodging the strikes from its razor-sharp beak and talons. The energy built inside Alexis, and she hoped she could hold onto it just a little longer.

The pterosaur took to the air again, manipulating its wings to hover awkwardly above her. It screeched, spraying her with hot saliva. She ducked a grab from its talons and scampered onto a bench to get a better shot.

Alexis grinned. "Just where I wanted you, sucker!" She unleashed the energy in a massive wave. The energy radiated outward from her, activating the portal and disintegrating the pterosaur in the process.

Alexis had another battle getting her legs to support her as she ran back to Gabriel through the falling ash. She scooped him into her arms with some difficulty.

"Come on, wake up!"

Gabriel muttered groggily but didn't wake.

Alexis sighed. "Fine, sleep through it all." She slid her hands under his armpits and dragged him onto the dais and through the portal.

Addix was waiting to take Gabriel from Alexis when she came through the portal into a cozy two-room cottage.

She handed her brother over and allowed her legs to take the vacation they so desperately wanted.

Gabriel stirred in Addix' arms as Alexis threw herself onto the couch in the corner of the main room. Addix peered at him closely. "Ah, good. He's waking up already." She placed him gently on the couch by Alexis to finish recovering and pulled a blanket over the both of them. "Well done, children. Sleep now."

Alexis yawned. "Are we in the new game now?"

"We are, but we won't begin until you and Gabriel have rested."

Alexis nodded. "Will you tell me about the game for my bedtime story?"

"Of course," Addix replied. "It's an old story, like Eve told you. There's a list of roles to choose from. You can be a mage, a fighter, a thief, a cleric…"

Alexis let out a soft snore.

Addix chuckled and tucked her in before taking out her tablet to review the game information. One of the character roles caught her eye. "Hmmm. I could be a Drow Ranger…"

CHAPTER TWENTY-TWO

Quarantined System, QBS *ArchAngel II*, Bridge

Bethany Anne paced the bridge with her hands behind her back. She glanced at the viewscreen for what could have been the hundredth time in the last two minutes and sighed impatiently. "ADAM, report. How are we fixed for position?"

"I have green lights across the board, Bethany Anne. The ships are in place and awaiting your orders."

Michael sat back in his chair and laced his hands.

Bethany Anne nodded once and stopped pacing. "Good. Let's see if they're the talkative kind. Open a channel, ADAM."

"Working on it," ADAM replied.

Bethany Anne raised an eyebrow. "They're not picking up?"

"Doesn't look like it."

"Well, damn. How rude."

"We have movement," Michael stated. He pointed to the

cloud of spheres that were detaching from the main structure and spreading out in all directions.

Tabitha sneered at the screen. "Guess that means early peace discussions are out the window."

Bethany Anne snorted. "Good. I always thought those discussions were boring, anyway. I'd rather leave the talking to those who enjoy it."

Kiel turned in his seat to face her. "They're definitely not the talking type. The spheres have just released all sort of nasty things. I'm getting confirmation of everything from straight-up kinetics to nuclear warheads. They'll be on us in less than thirty minutes."

Bethany Anne was warmed by Kiel's literal take on her words. She put a hand on his shoulder and chuckled. "Never change, Kiel."

For his part, Kiel looked at her blankly, then shrugged and turned back to his station. He'd stopped being embarrassed about being caught out by his Queen's wordplay long ago.

Bethany Anne walked to the front of the bridge and clapped her hands, all humor gone from her voice. "You heard Kiel. We have less than thirty minutes to prepare a suitable welcome for these fuckers. Let's go!"

Fifteen minutes later they were speeding away from the ship in Black Eagles.

Bethany Anne opened the comm. "Everyone good?"

"Roger," John answered for himself and Tabitha.

"Let's fuck some shit up," Scott commented from his and Darryl's Pod.

"Ready," Gabrielle and Eric answered in unison.

"Ready to turn tail if you need me to," Jean grumped from the backup ship.

Bethany Anne grinned at Michael, who raised his eyebrows in amusement and went back to turning his mystery box over and over in his hands. "Quit your bitching, Jean. I can hear you rolling your eyes from here."

"Bite me, my Queen," came the reply.

"Love you too," she shot back. "Everyone else, best of luck and I'll see you all on that ship." She turned to Michael again. "You need to bleed on it."

Michael's face dropped. "I would have gotten it by myself. I was enjoying the mystery." He sighed and pricked the end of his finger with his canine, then smeared the resulting drop of blood on the box. It opened with a soft click. "Now half the fun is gone."

She shrugged. "Save the mystery for when we're not about to land on an alien ship with no idea what's waiting for us. Open the box. The fun is just getting started, my love."

He lifted the lid and took out the velvet drawstring bag inside. "Heavy."

Bethany Anne nodded distractedly, her focus on getting their Pod through the battlefield unscathed. "Open it. We're halfway to the ship already."

Michael pulled the string and took out the gauntlets within. A look of appreciation crossed his face as he admired the intricate filigree worked through the black leather. "They are beautiful, my love." He pulled them on. "From the same creature as my favorite boots of yours?"

Bethany Anne nodded. "I made sure to save enough of the hide for Jean to make them. It took a while to add the special feature since it's so difficult to do anything with the leather."

Michael flexed his fingers inside the gauntlets, feeling a slight surge of Etheric energy leave his fingertips. He looked at Bethany Anne quizzically.

"Now you don't need my help to call lightning."

He leaned over and kissed her. "Thank you. They're perfect."

A proximity alarm cut off any further thanks Michael may have offered. Bethany Anne turned back to the Pod controls as the EI dealt with the incoming kinetics. "It's getting intense out there."

"You have a gift for understatement." Michael scrolled through the fleet data. "The dreadnoughts are laying it down pretty thick."

"They're doing some good work. Look at the spheres drop." She slowed the Pod as it crossed into the shadow of the behemoth. "Are we ready to kick the doors in?" she asked over the comm.

The sound of six rifles being cocked simultaneously filled her ears.

"Ready when you are," John deadpanned.

Bethany Anne cracked up, any pre-battle tension she might have had shattered. "Be careful out there, all of you."

"We will," Tabitha promised.

"You too," Gabrielle added.

"See you all inside." She closed the channel and turned to Michael. "Shall we dance by the light of the pale moon?"

The alien ship grew closer in their viewscreen. The closer they got, the less like a comet the structure looked. It was more spherical in shape underneath the cloaking. The sphere's surface was made up mostly of shipwrecks packed in together in a way that made Bethany Anne's head hurt. "It's like somebody made a Death Star from junked cars," she remarked.

Michael pointed out a group of cracked, dead ships floating along the curvature of the sphere. "Are those our missing Noel-ni ships?"

Bethany Anne scrutinized the floating wrecks. "Could be. John and Tabitha are coming in from that direction. Have them send some drones in to check it out."

John brought the Pod in past the drifting Noel-ni ships and released the drones.

Tabitha pulled a face at the dark hulks as they left them behind. The ships emitted no signals, and they picked up no power signatures. The hulls were twisted in places. "It looks like they were torn open. I don't think anyone could survive that."

John grunted. "If they're just holed up, then we'll get them out of there when we're done. Okay, brace yourself."

Tabitha grinned. "Time to deliver that door-kicking you wanted?"

John smirked. "You betcha. And since we can't find a door, we'll have to make our own." He mashed the button to send a complement of pucks at the rapidly approaching wall of wrecks.

The space beyond the twisted, blackened metal was pitch-dark.

Gabrielle and Eric were first-in since they had the closest point of entry. They stepped over the debris left by their big entrance with their new rifles raised and ready. They were in a wide workroom with computer stations spread throughout. They activated their HUDs and a window appeared at the top of their vision, ready for the video feeds from the other teams.

One by one they came on as the others breached the ship.

Eric and Gabrielle searched the room quietly while they waited for Bethany Anne and Michael to breach the far side.

"I can't believe Jean did this." Gabrielle indicated a small-but-heavy storage tank mounted on her rifle. "If it weren't for my vampire strength, I wouldn't even be able to lift it."

"Just be glad she likes you so much," Eric told her. "She didn't give *me* a flamethrower."

Scott's voice barked over the comm. "We have contact, and oh my good lord these fuckers are weird-looking." There was a burst from his and Darryl's rifles. "They seem to die just fine all the same."

He panned his camera down to show them the attacker, a mechanoid with eight deadly limbs placed in incongruous spots around its torso. The cameras that protruded from the top of its body waved weakly and gave up.

"It makes me a little worried that the archetype for this species' robot technology is arachnid," Bethany Anne muttered to the channel.

Tabitha's response was a bit muted. "I don't know what that means, but we have them too."

Eric looked up, hearing an ominous scratching.

"Us too," Gabrielle confirmed. She brought up her rifle and fired at the wall by the exit on the far left. The high-velocity flechettes passed through the wall like butter, and a metallic screech filled the room.

"It means," Bethany Anne told them between shots, "that people tend to make things in their own image."

Eric darted over and took out the two arachnobots Gabrielle's blind shooting had missed.

They collapsed in a shower of sparks and were still.

Eric shouldered his rifle as they walked up the corridor. "That wasn't too bad."

Gabrielle rolled her eyes, hearing differently. She unslung her rifle and flipped the switch for the flamethrower. "You just had to say something, huh?"

Eric gave her a puzzled look but readied his rifle, since he knew better than to dismiss his wife's instincts.

Then he heard the echo of a multitude of approaching feet.

"Now I *really* wish I had the flamethrower," he bitched as the lights went out at the other end of the corridor, covered by the arachnobots on every inch of the walls and ceiling. He turned the dial on his rifle to switch to electrified scattershot. "Or an EMP. Now *that* would have been useful."

CHAPTER TWENTY-THREE

Quarantined System, Inside the Perimeter

The High Tortuga fleet had the alien ship surrounded on all sides. It sent out wave after wave of spheres to retaliate against the heavy pounding it was taking from the dreadnoughts.

The dreadnoughts had disgorged their smaller ships and fighter Pods in response, and the void was repeatedly lit with silent explosions, high-velocity kinetics, and arcing plasma fire going both ways.

In short, it was as if Hell had come visiting without the volume having been turned up.

Pilot Brock Sanders darted in and out amid the chaos, dropping mines which would activate if a ship passed that didn't perform the correct electronic handshake.

The sheer scale of the destruction completely awed Brock. He'd seen some major shit, but nothing as big as this.

The space all around him was littered with defunct

spheres and pieces of shattered Pods. The dreadnoughts held the line, steadily beating back the larger spheres from a distance while the smaller ships like Brock's did the up close and personal work.

"We're getting to the end of this load," the EI informed him.

"Let's swing back, then," Brock decided. "We'll grab another load and finish it on the next run." His Pod suddenly lurched. "What was that?"

There was no response from the EI.

Brock saw the second kinetic coming. His eyes widened in the brief second between the realization he was going to die and his Pod being blown to pieces.

Inside the alien ship, Bethany Anne and Michael stood back-to-back at the T-junction in the arachnobot-infested corridor. The inner ship was crawling with masses of the spider-legged bots, forcing them to battle for every step they gained.

"Every turn we make, we find more of the creepy fuckers," Bethany Anne bitched. She blasted the seething mass with a volley of energy balls, and the next wave crawled over the jerking legs of the ones she'd just taken out.

"Are these our aliens, then?" Michael wondered as he waved his hand and sent a web of lightning out to disable more of the robots. "Surely something so simple could not have created all this?" He flicked the hand toward the ceiling and the arachnobots rained down and landed on the floor, twitching with residual electricity.

"I don't know. ADAM, do you have access yet?"

>> *I am almost in control of the secondary systems, but there is a large area at the center of the ship that I cannot yet access. I suspect you'll find what you're looking for there. Sending directions now.*<<

Bethany Anne flung out a wall of Etheric energy that traveled down all three corridors and finished the bots off. She glanced at Michael while wiping sweaty hair out of her face. "Did you get that?"

He nodded. "I did, and sent the directions to the other teams and told them to meet us there," he finished. His eye caught a movement; one of the arachnobots twitching. He blew it up with a narrow streak of lightning before it could move again.

Bethany Anne grinned. "Come on. As much fun as playing with your new toy is, I don't think we've reached our true foe yet."

Michael flexed his fingers in the gauntlets as they walked along the center corridor, feeling the transfer of Etheric energy from his body to the intricate circuitry in the leather. "They really are one of your more inspired gifts."

She shrugged and pressed ahead. "All they do is focus your ability," she explained, eyes darting everywhere to make sure none of the little buggers sneaked up on her.

The path laid out by ADAM led them to a set of fifteen-foot-wide and thirty-foot-high blast doors. "We'll wait for the others here."

"You don't need to, we're here." Tabitha strolled down the corridor with her enormous rifle balanced on her shoulder. John was just behind her, and the others arrived shortly after him.

Darryl looked at the blast doors, one eyebrow raised. "Who wants to knock?"

"Allow me." Tabitha twiddled the dial on her rifle. "I've been looking for an excuse to give Gracie her head." She braced her feet and fitted the oversized rifle stock into her shoulder.

"You look a little nervous," Michael remarked. "Have you tested this weapon?" He shook his head at her incredulous look.

Tabitha shrugged. "Consider this the test, 'cuz I haven't fired her on this setting, and I'm expecting a little kickback. Here it goes."

The rifle uttered a short, sharp whine, and a 10-foot-tall melting hole appeared in the blast door.

"ShiIIIIIIiit!" BAM!

They all watched Tabitha fly backward. She landed on her ass and slid another ten feet or so before she regained control.

Tabitha got up and retrieved her rifle, then stalked past them toward the glowing hole with her chin held high and her finger raised as she ignored everyone. "Not a word. Not a single *fucking* word…"

Bethany Anne followed her through the hole, barely managing to keep it together and not laugh. "Come on, it's not as bad as the time you walked off a building," she offered.

"Or that *other* time you walked off a building," Scott chipped in as he emerged from the hole.

John added, "Or the time you tripped over the cable in the landing bay."

Tabitha narrowed her eyes and waved the finger she was giving them. "Haven't we got better things to do, like find these sonsofbitches and teach them not to fuck around in our backyard?" She hooked her arm through her rifle strap and pushed it around to her back, then drew her pistols. "Jean asked us all to give them hell from her, but we can't do that if we're all gonna stand around the whole time talking about literally the only three mistakes I've made in my whole life."

She was saved from Bethany Anne's snarky reply by the attack that came out of nowhere. The alien dropped from the ceiling, knocking Tabitha to the floor. It came at her, baring row after row of razor-sharp teeth. "Oh, you ugly-assed fuck!" She kicked it back and rolled to her feet before it could recover and jump her again.

Michael raised his hand, and a bright blue line of lightning left his finger and slammed into the alien. It screeched and pitched forward, almost knocking Tabitha over again before it fell face-down on the floor.

Tabitha eyed Michael, eyebrow raised as he shrugged. She looked down and poked the alien with her foot, then flipped it onto its back with a harder shove.

They stood around the twitching alien with its chest blown open and its spindly metal legs waving uselessly. The alien most closely resembled a grub, if grubs had eight eyes, were blue, and had merged with technology to get around better.

The grub on the floor was wracked with pain, its dying convulsions twisting its limp body and jerking the mechanical legs around in a way that made the merging of flesh and machine even more disturbing.

Gabrielle gagged a little.

Bethany Anne said what they were all thinking. "What the shiny fuck is *that*?"

Gabrielle readied her flamethrower. "I don't know, but there's more of them."

Outer Quarantine Zone, QBS *Valiant*

The EI Valiant broadcast loud and clear from every speaker on the ship. "This is the order to evacuate. All hands to the ship's bays. This is *not* a drill."

Captain Petra Deveaux stumbled against the railing of the platform from which she was watching the last evacuees scramble into their Pods when the ship shuddered from a third impact.

The evacuation had been triggered when the *Valiant* had taken a hit which had disabled the life support systems. The surrounding dreadnoughts were providing what cover they could while the crew made their escape.

Petra, however, wasn't ready to give up on her ship just yet, or on Valiant. She was pissed as hell that she was out of the fight, and the urge to stay with the ship until the bitter end was overwhelming.

"How are you holding up, Captain?" Valiant's voice in her ear was a comfort.

"How do you *think* I'm holding up? My ship is only good as a diversion and you are about to die making some big heroic sacrifice, and there's not a damn thing I can do about it!"

Valiant cut in as the ship shuddered again. "Captain, please think logically. I am backed up, and will continue to update my backup up until the final moment. I'll be up again in no time, and a ship can be replaced. You cannot, Petra, so please allow me to do my duty and protect the people of this ship. We will fight together another day."

Petra sighed, her fingers tapping the railing. "Okay."

Twenty-two seconds later she made her escape from the *Valiant* and watched from a safe distance while Valiant turned the beleaguered ship and made a run for the enemy line to give the rest of the fleet a chance to regroup.

"Give 'em hell for the rest of us, Valiant," she murmured as the shields around her ship flared brightly.

CHAPTER TWENTY-FOUR

The alien grubs poured from every door along the wide corridor. These were armored and held weapons in each of their four hands. They moved to block the corridor, brandishing their weapons at the humans with guttural snarls.

Bethany Anne tilted her head, looking past the grubs to the door at the other end of the corridor. It was twice as big as the one they'd come through, and she sensed it was also much thicker. *ADAM, can you get that door open while we clear this corridor?*

>>I'm working on it,<< he replied. >>I don't know what their technology is based on, but it's every bit as good as ours.<<

Just do what you can. I'll take care of the rest.

The grubs attacked. Bethany Anne gathered Etheric energy even as she reshaped her nails into talons. She threw the energy at the closest grubs and sliced up the front of another in two easy steps. The grubs rushed her, and she took out six more of them with another energy blast.

The others fought around her, islands of destruction in a sea of dead and dying grubs. The noise was incredible. She dialed out the screeching and focused on working her way up the corridor toward the door.

Michael made his way through the crush, his progress marked by bright flashes and flying, burning grubs. *You weren't going to run ahead without your backup, were you?*

She swept a hand and released the energy, making skittles out of the grubs around them. *I was not. ADAM hasn't managed to crack the door yet.* She flung another volley of energy balls at a particularly large and aggressive grub. It roared in her face but retracted its head when she roared right back at it with her eyes red and her gleaming teeth exposed.

She thrust a hand through its carapace and dragged her claws through its insides, then kicked it away and moved onto the next. **ADAM, get that door open!**

>>**About that...**<<

Bethany Anne slashed and kicked the oncoming grubs, which were finally dwindling in number. *You can't open it?*

>>**Not so much. Sorry.**<<

She rolled her eyes. "Do I have to do everything around here?"

Michael frowned. "He can't open it?"

Bethany Anne shook her head. "Nope. Everyone, cover me. I need to concentrate." She held her hands up. She could feel Scott, Darryl, and John regroup around her, facing out as they took care of those trying to assault her. Bethany Anne's hands grew bright, her training time with

TOM coming to mind as she opened a small portal and fed the released energy into her efforts.

Bethany Anne shot a stream of burning Etheric energy to clear a path to the massive door, then stood in front of the door and gave herself a little pep talk as she shook herself. "No big deal. It's only the most Etheric energy you've ever attempted to control, and it's totally not going to tear you apart."

It is *not* going to tear you apart, Bethany Anne, TOM chided. **You have practiced for this, and you are ready. Now blast that bitch.**

Bethany Anne snorted, but she shook off her doubt and raised her palms toward the door. *Okay,* **now** *I'm ready.*

TOM chuckled. **My work here is done.**

Thank you. I needed that.

One thing life with you has taught me is that a little humor goes a long way in these situations.

True. She stopped talking and paid attention to her breathing. When it was deep and regular, she reached for the Etheric and began to pull once more, spooling the energy up until the raw power of it filled her almost to bursting.

Good, now compress the energy. *Trust* your instincts.

She tightened her hold and willed the energy to harden almost, drawing in more to feed the growing mass she held just outside of reality until it felt just right. "Fire in the hole!" she yelled. The energy left her hands and collided with the door with a blinding flash of white light and a deep, reverberating *CLANG!*

The shockwave sent a ripple through the ship and the floor bucked unexpectedly, making everyone stumble.

Bethany Anne and Michael recovered their footing first and immediately headed for the door, which was now less of a door and more of a glowing, superheated portal to the room beyond.

They entered the large amphitheater-style room with the others close behind.

"Holy shit!" Scott exclaimed as he ducked a droplet of molten metal.

Tabitha dodged as he jumped back to avoid another. "Watch out for the glowy red stuff, superstar."

Scott gave her the finger and moved off to keep watch over Bethany Anne and Michael.

Bethany Anne looked down at the "stage," where two aliens sat working under a semi-translucent dome, oblivious to the intrusion. They had four arms, eight eyes attached to stalks on their heads, and grub bodies.

Ugh, exactly what I was afraid of. TOM, do you know anything about these aliens? What's up with them not noticing their front door just got blown in?"

They are a mental species, he explained. **They have enormous skill with the Etheric, which is how all of this is working together so well. They are not concerned with this reality, other than how they can manipulate it to serve them.**

Michael adjusted his position to get a better view of the aliens. *Do they have any links to the Kurtherians?*

No, TOM replied. **Just your garden variety shit-bags who love to take over other races.**

Must be Kurtherian cousins, then, Bethany Anne quipped. *Of the Seven, not the Five,* she added quickly. She created a ball of energy and threw it at the dome to test the strength of the barrier. "Couldn't just be easy, huh?" she wondered aloud when it had no effect other than to draw the attention of the aliens.

Michael wasn't there to reply.

"And you talk about *me* running off without backup," she grumbled.

She looked around, seeing everyone *but* Michael. "Where did you—" She was dropped to her knees by a sudden stabbing sensation in her brain. The others were on the floor around her, clutching their heads as the aliens pressed their psionic attack.

Michael was still nowhere to be seen.

Bethany Anne screamed her rage at the intrusion through gritted teeth and pushed the aliens from her mind. She forced herself to her feet and clenched her fists until the dizziness receded. "Nice try, assholes."

The aliens were taken aback. They chittered to each other animatedly, clearly fascinated by Bethany Anne.

The stalks on their heads turned as one to scrutinize her.

"Such power," the first crooned. "*New* powers... So raw, so talented..."

The other cut in. "So *tasty*. Can you imagine what her mind will taste like?"

Her translation software handled the conversation, although by that point she wished it hadn't bothered.

They chuckled, and Bethany Anne was hammered with a much harder attack. She screamed, barely able to fight back as the aliens ravaged her with wave after increasing wave of pain.

TOM stepped in. He blocked Bethany Anne's pain and

placed himself between her mind and the aliens. **Oh, no, you didn't just threaten to eat my friend's mind.** He unleashed an attack of his own, giving Bethany Anne time to recover.

The aliens recoiled. "A *Kurtherian?*"

Damn right, a Kurtherian. However, I am not the deadliest being in this room at the moment. Now, *die.*

The aliens pulled themselves together and launched a fresh attack to counter TOM's.

"There are two of us," one pointed out. "And only one of you. Kurtherian or not, your host is damaged."

The silky smooth voice of death spoke from behind them.

"His host's *husband* is not," it said.

Michael turned to Myst and began to probe the alien dome. It had a perfect seal, preventing him from getting inside no matter how thin he spread himself. When the aliens began their attack, the dome relaxed just a fraction. It was enough for him to start to push himself through the barrier a few molecules at a time.

The dome weakened further when they focused on Bethany Anne. It killed him to see her in pain, but he knew that the quickest way to end her suffering was to get through the barrier and tear the hearts out of the alien grubs.

TOM's attack gave him the opportunity he'd been waiting for.

The dome flickered for less than a tenth of a second,

but the pressure he was exerting over the entire surface caused his molecules to plummet to the floor inside the dome when the resistance was removed.

Michael pulled himself into a cloud behind the aliens just as they were talking proudly about having damaged his love. He solidified and, having taken off his gauntlets, reached into their backs with two fully clawed hands.

When he pulled them out, they held two dripping, steaming lumps of flesh that were still half-attached to the insides.

"I don't know if you need these," Michael hissed into their ears as their eyes opened in shock. "But I know I have your attention now. I'll just take these until you can prove you won't attack my wife again... *Just kidding.*" He ripped their organs out the rest of the way, and they slumped to the floor. "You can die. I really don't care." The dome failed and he dropped the organs with a look of distaste, then noticed Bethany Anne's eyes opening.

Michael looked around as the team started to get to their feet. John and Gabrielle were up first and checked on the others while he headed to Bethany Anne's side.

Quarantined System (twelve hours later)

Bethany Anne stalked irritably ten feet ahead of the demolition teams as she led them through the alien ship to talk about dismantling it.

"Go through this place and strip it of anything that looks even remotely important." She tore another strip off the roll of tape she was carrying to mark items she wanted to be sent straight to Jean's lab on the *ArchAngel II* and pressed it to the console the aliens had been working at. "You have twelve hours, since in fourteen hours I want there to be a fuck-load of *nothing at all* here. Do you understand?"

She dismissed the teams and continued her walk-through, stopping when she got to the loading bays to allow herself a minute to observe the bustle. Ships moved in and out of the massive hangar doors in turn, and shuttles zipped in with a bunch of people and out again loaded with machinery for the return.

The first demolition team came in, then went out again. They had captured some of the bigger chunks of the battleship and pulled them into the hangar, leaving other pieces to be blown by the explosives teams. The retrieved pieces had been laid out in an open area, and there were people all around working on them.

Michael wandered over to Bethany Anne to watch the proceedings with her. "What are they doing?" he asked, indicating a few of the workers who appeared to be painting the pieces of wreckage.

Bethany Anne grinned and tapped the side of her nose with a finger. "That would be telling, wouldn't it?" She slapped his ass and walked off. "I have a call with my dad. I'll tell you about the painting later."

Michael let her go without pressing for an answer. He had a secret of his own to check on. He made his way to a secluded part of the ship and opened an Etheric connection to Eve.

"How are the children? he asked the moment Eve appeared.

"They're doing extremely well," she told him proudly. "They have completed the island scenario and rested for the night. They are about to become the first virtual reality players in this system to put on their helmets, grab their swords or magic wands, and create new characters for Dragons and Caves."

Michael smiled at Eve's excited spiel. "Little do they know that their real training is about to commence." He snickered. "Make sure they can beat their first couple of levels quickly. I want them suckered into the endorphins of leveling up."

Eve snorted. "Are you trying to teach me to suck eggs?"

Michael laughed. "I apologize, Eve. I should respect the true genius you represent."

"Damn right," she stated. "OH! They are picking their character classes now. I have to go before Addix takes the one I want. See you when you get back." She cut the connection without another word.

Michael frowned. "Dammit, now I don't get to be there when they take their first virtual steps."

———

Bethany Anne tapped the table as she listened to the General's report. She didn't miss the look of concern her father gave her when he saw the dark rings under her eyes. "I'm okay, Dad," she reassured him. "So, how did it go from your end?"

"When the satellites hit the system, all they found was

smoking debris strewn for kilometers." He let slip a small smile. "The Leath and the Noel-ni are going apeshit wondering who did this."

Bethany Anne shrugged. "Let them wonder."

The concerned look returned to Lance's face. "I trust there is nothing there to pin this to you?"

She smirked. "Not a sausage. We cleaned up the system, but we left a few clues to divert from looking too hard at it."

Lance raised an eyebrow. "Clues? To what?"

"The Dread Pirate Roberts Dark Empire Squadron, of course," she told him. "High Tortuga has come out victorious..." She thought of those who hadn't made it through the battle. "Although we took some hard losses as well. Next time you come here and bring my brother, I'll show you the video."

They spoke a little more, then Lance excused himself.

"I have to smooth some ruffled feathers," he explained. He hesitated before signing off. "I am sorry for the losses the High Tortuga fleet suffered. Thank you all for your sacrifice."

Bethany Anne nodded soberly. "We may not be wanted, but we're not asking for recognition either. We will be there in the darkness, watching and waiting. Some of those who whisper will have whispered the truth. One of these days—may it be a long time in the future—the Queen Bitch will be back."

Lance shrugged. "What will be, will be. For now, it is an enigma that will occupy them for a while. It helps me keep their focus away from all the other shit I'm pulling."

"Whatever you need, Dad. You know that."

"You too, pumpkin."

Michael wandered in just in time to wave to Lance before he signed off.

Bethany Anne took in his smile and his practically jaunty posture and was instantly suspicious. "What are you up to?"

"Nothing," he told her. "Just making sure the children are studying."

"The children love studying. Why would you need to check?"

Michael held his hands up. "Can't a loving father miss his children while he's away from them?" He sighed, affronted, then turned and left.

"Hmmm." The spring in his step told a different story than the pout he'd given her, but she decided to let it pass. "Don't look a gift horse in the mouth," she muttered as he left again. "He's taking on the responsibility for the children. I should be happy, excited, and beyond joyous that he's so involved..."

Then why aren't you? Tom asked as she headed out.

"Because he's up to something. Any time that man is *that* happy, he's up to something."

High Tortuga, Space Fleet Base, The Dome

Bethany Anne dropped her robe in preparation for the training session and took her usual cross-legged pose on the mat with her hands resting loosely on her knees and her chin on her chest. She had just begun the breathing part of the process when ADAM interrupted.

>>Bethany Anne?<<

What's up, ADAM?

>>We have received a data burst from one of the scout explorers, the Loralei.<<

And?

>>The scout ship was attacked by an unknown entity, and as far as I can tell the ship was destroyed. The EI managed to get a partial scan of the attacker, but it didn't make it to us intact.<<

Bethany Anne opened an audio-only link to the Security Pit. She wasn't going to get dressed just to make a quick call. "This is Bethany Anne."

Jennifer chuckled. "I know, my Queen. I would recognize your voice anywhere."

"ADAM told you it was me calling, right?"

Jennifer's chuckle deepened into a laugh. "Okay, you got me. What can I do for you?"

Bethany Anne dropped the smile. "I want a team to go out to the coordinates ADAM is about to send. One of the scout fleet has run into difficulty."

"On it now. Anything else?"

"No, thank you, Jennifer." Bethany Anne shut down the link. This looked to be another thread of the mystery that she could pull on, and maybe it would be the one that unraveled this whole plot and gave her the understanding of the higher workings of the parts of the galaxy she hadn't yet reached. "Could be a simple retrieve and return, or something a little meatier. What do you guys think? Maybe it's the same people we just fought."

>>It doesn't seem likely. Loralei didn't report seeing any spheres when she was attacked.<<

Bethany Anne pressed her lips together and considered

the possibilities. Eventually, she shrugged. "Well, whoever it is, life just got a little more interesting." With that announcement, she settled back in for her training session. "We're going to work on those mind attacks. No pain, no gain, TOM. We're going to keep at this until I get it."

She opened her eyes in the darkness. "I don't want to be taken out so easily *next time*."

EPILOGUE

Immersive Recreation and Training Scenario, Dungeons and Caves, Base Cottage (The Next Morning)

Alexis smoothed the front of her elaborately-embroidered robe with a hand and shuffled the hem with her foot. She looked up at Eve doubtfully. "Won't this get in the way when we fight?"

Eve smirked. "Oh, but the mage does not fight with her body. She fights with her mind." She reached out and plucked a gnarled wooden staff with a ruby topper out of the air. "Here, now you just need one more thing..."

Alexis took the staff from her with a puzzled frown. "What?"

Eve held out her hand with a flourish and gave Alexis the hat that appeared. "Perfect. *Now* you look like a mage."

Alexis gave the strange hat a look and put it on. "What exactly does a mage do, and why did you suggest I choose it?" She took a closer look at the staff, which felt a little tingly in her hand. She thought she saw a spark in the center of the ruby.

"You gave me the idea," Eve told her. "I had not anticipated your solution to the pterosaur obstacle. I had fully expected you to use the environment to your advantage instead."

Alexis tilted her head back when the hat slipped over her eyes. "You mean the rockfall above the portal? I didn't see that until I was dragging Gabriel up the dais steps."

Eve's mouth twitched. "But you *did* see it. And you took to channeling energy like a duck to water. It will be easy for you to transfer the knowledge to your role as a mage."

Alexis frowned, remembering the close shave they'd had by the river in the last scenario. "So we can use magic here?"

Gabriel came out from behind the curtain, plucking at the scarf that covered his face. "Why do we need to wear a costume for this? Our atmosuits were fine." He held his cloak out from his body and turned from side to side. "This is pretty cool, though."

Addix shuffled uncomfortably into the room, being careful not to knock any of them with the bulky spiked armor she wore. "I have to disagree. It is uncomfortable."

Eve shrugged. She swished her kimono, to which she had added a hood and shining armor plates, and looked Addix over. "No, that won't do at all." She tilted her head and closed her eyes for a moment, then snapped her fingers.

Addix started in surprise when the generic armor disappeared and was replaced by something that made the most of her deadly Ixtali nature. The new armor was so black it sucked the light from around Addix, and it fit her like a second skin—except where it curved away from both elbows and all four ankles to form blades. She flexed her limbs and nodded. "Very good, Eve."

"Cooool," Gabriel breathed. "Aunt Eve, next time I want to be the fighter."

"It's not too late to switch class," Eve offered.

Gabriel shook his head. "No, thank you, Aunt Eve. I reviewed the information this time, and I want to be the thief."

Alexis stamped her foot. "The game information! I didn't read it...again!"

Eve shook her head. "I didn't want you reading it for this game, Alexis."

Alexis rolled her eyes. "Is this a nuance thing again?"

"Kind of feels like this scene should have a stirring orchestral piece playing," Eve commented.

Addix gave her a puzzled glance and went back to looking over the land below the ridge they'd climbed to get a better view of the area. The children were close behind, Alexis using her staff as a walking stick to counter the weight of her robes and Gabriel keeping pace with his sister.

They came to a stop beside the adults, and all four drank in the raging battle that was occurring below. The land heaved with the mass of many species, some that neither Alexis nor Gabriel had seen before.

"Who are they?" Alexis asked. "Why are they fighting?"

"It was in the backstory for the scenario," Gabriel supplied. He pointed out a band of fighters in the center of the battlefield. They fought from the backs of enormous silver-horned stags with swords and bows and spells. "The tall ones are elves, and they're fighting the orcs. The good humans and the dwarves are on the elves' side. All the others are on the orcs' side."

Wherever the elves went, orcs and their allies fell.

"Maybe I'll be an elf next time," Alexis mused.

"Come, children," Eve urged. She led them along the ridge to a crumbling watchtower which looked directly onto the battlefield.

"Now remember," Eve cautioned, "you will feel the pain of any injuries you take, and you can die in this scenario." She turned to face the children. "This battle is just the scene. The objective is to reach the other side, by whatever method you like."

Gabriel narrowed his eyes at the fray. "By ourselves?"

Addix shook her head. "No, Gabriel. Eve and I will be there to provide a certain level of protection."

"However," Eve cut in, "we will only move as you and Alexis direct."

Alexis looked up from the ruby on her staff, which was glowing. "I think I have the hang of this magic thing now."

"Great," Gabriel told her, looking at the sky and then behind himself. "Was that a *dragon* I just heard?"

High Tortuga, Space Fleet Base, The Dome
Bethany Anne pushed the plastic curtain aside and

stalked over to the door she felt the children's presence behind. She opened the door and saw Michael and Eve watching the screen wall.

The screen wall that showed her children engaged in battle with a dragon, of all fucking things.

"Michael, what is going on here?"

Michael turned. "Excellent, you are just in time. The children are done with their lessons for the day."

Three of the four Pod-docs opened and Alexis and Gabriel spilled out, chattering animatedly as they climbed over the sides.

Alexis' eyes were open wide. "You were *awesome* when you stole the elf's bow and shot the orc's throat out through its mouth."

Gabriel was just as full of praise for his sister. "I thought the best part was when you used Aunt Addix as a spring-board to jump up and stab that cyclops right in its eye with your staff. When you let the magic go it danced!"

The twins caught sight of their mom with their father. "Mommy's home!" they cried in unison. They ran over to hug their mother as Addix clambered out of her pod.

"We missed you!" Gabriel cried.

"Even though we had fun playing Daddy's and Eve's game," Alexis added.

Bethany Anne gave Michael a pointed look and gathered Alexis and Gabriel to her. "Mommy missed you both so much!" She held them close and kissed their heads. "How about some real food, and you can tell me about all of your adventures while I was away."

They scampered toward their quarters, with Bethany

Anne and Michael walking behind. Eve called to them as they reached the door.

"I've sent the review of the children's scores from the scenario. You're going to be so proud of them! I know I was."

FINIS

DEUCES WILD

Have you read the Deuces Wild series yet? Book One is Beyond The Frontier.

Don't miss this rip-roaring, bar brawling adventure series as Nickie, and The Kurtherian Gambit's original Ranger 2, Tabitha, try to save the frontier from slavery, arms dealing and the 'Skaine' of the universe.

Available at Amazon

THANK YOU for reading this story, and our *Author Notes* in the back!

There is SO MUCH going on that sometimes I don't know what I've said and who I have told it to. In one week, I'll be joining tens of thousands of fans at Worldcon 76 in San Jose, California (my first time.) I'm going there to see what it is like, and to promote the company a bit with the SFWA members and generally to check it out.

On the 20th of this month, I fly to Beijing, China to visit the book fair they have going and to travel (check it out) for future ideas. The challenge (for me) is that I'm so picky with my food (pretty much meat and potatoes, with the meat being beef usually), I suspect I'm going to lose some weight on the trip. Not that me losing weight is a bad thing, I have plenty I can afford to give away.

Almost all books are a collaborative effort. (Except my first two—I tried to get a proofreader by Love Lost, I think, but that guy only made it worse. So how 'collaborative' can a book be when you support person undermines your effort? I don't know, that sounds like an existential editor question.) Existential questions aside, I want to point out why (pretty much) all Michael Anderle books are *productions* of Michael Anderle books more and more (besides the obvious collaborations).

Children

Now, I have three children. But for this Kurtherian Endgame book I needed to bring in children who are *really, really young*, and I am going to hit fifty-one in about a month.

(Don't listen to Martha Carr when she says 'Happy Birthday!' next month, because she gets it wrong. Last year, I had to go through a WHOLE WEEK of people telling me Happy Birthday because she announced my birthday a week early. She still finds that shit funny as hell.)

Anyway, my kids are 26, and 19, 19 (on the 22nd of August.) I haven't had to work with younger kids in many, many years. Also, I don't channel them very well. I looked forward to pulling together this book with a sense of dread. "Children? What the hell am I going to do with children?"

Thank GOD for people who help me make these books happen!

Natale Roberts

For those who don't know Natale Roberts (She did books 03 and 04 in the Etheric Academy series writing as N. D. Roberts.) Nat was a MAJOR help helping me get this book done. Her insights into the kids and creating their personalities was off-the-charts helpful, as well as many other efforts with the writing. Even while she was dealing with additional projects, she was monumentally helpful in pulling this book together.

Beta Readers

We have changed how we do Beta Reading and I want to SHOUT OUT to the Beta Readers for dealing with the changes. It hasn't been easy, and I understand that. I appreciate Lynne Stiegler and the team(s) of Beta Readers, Editors, JIT folks and everyone working to deliver as clean a book as we can with these crazy freaking deadlines.

Artists

I want to thank Andrew Dobell, Jude <redacted I think upon request>, and Jeff Brown for their help with the art. Jude pulled together Bethany Anne's armor and pose, Andrew merged the armor with our Helen Diaz's photos and then created the *whole* rest of the cover, and Jeff has helped with creating the 3D ship you see at the top (Arch-Angel 2.)

Operations

Stephen Campbell and Jami Crumpton help keep the back end of the operations (publishing, notifying, emailing, Facebook updates, responding and fixing typos, working with some marketing and other things) in the books. There is so much more that goes on that Steve's group manages, that I'm sure I am forgetting something (or many somethings, actually.)

Fans

In my mind, it goes without saying that you, the fans and readers, are a major aspect of doing these stories (not only *The Kurtherian Endgame*, but all of our series. From your support purchasing (and reading on Kindle Unlimited) to the kind reviews (we always need them) to reaching out on Facebook and Reddit. Yes, I've actually been on Reddit recently. Scares me shitless. Not that I mind chatting with folks, but it brings out of me an argumentative side that frankly, I don't need to even remotely give into. Further, they have this *popular* trending area on Reddit that has caused me to take productive time and replace it with 'oh, that was funny! Let's see what's next!' time.

It wasn't much of a help. Kind of like drinking Coca-Cola isn't a good way to acquire calories, but I like it so much I do it anyway. There! That's the message. Reading the popular Reddit posts is a way to lose my nutritious time and replace it with sugar-calorie laden time.

That metaphor was so much more interesting in my mind.

Movies

Nothing has happened (of substance) on the movie front. We have had people interested, but it seems that Hollywood doesn't want to put much money down in the beginning. Since The Kurtherian Gambit series sells very, very well, often the money offered (if there is any) is equivalent to a few days or a couple of weeks of sales.

Yes, you read that correctly. Hollywood is offering tiny amounts of money to lock up the IP, and we aren't willing to do it. I am working (every so freaking slowly) in the background on 3D efforts, so perhaps in the future, LMBPN will just have to do it ourselves.

Baby steps, I keep reminding myself. Baby steps.

NEXT BOOK WON'T TAKE 3 MONTHS.

This book took about twelve weeks to come out (May 14th to August 10th). I am looking for (I really hope) the next Kurtherian Endgame book to be about 6 to 8 weeks, tops.

MAYBE EVEN SOONER!

(Did you hear a 'squee'? If you did, that wasn't me, I promise. As a fifty-ish year-old man, I don't *squee*.) (Editor's note: He does too. I have heard him)

I've got help on this series (where before I did most of everything except the editing stuff) and we are kicking ass. To that end, I'm working to pull the production of the Bethany Anne books down to something almost reasonable, and I *sincerely* appreciate you allowing me the six months to get my other projects off the ground and slowing Bethany Anne production down to make that happen.

I am focused on trying (I can't promise accomplishing, yet) but trying to get Bethany Anne books out on a faster schedule.

Ad Aeternitatem,

Michael Anderle

CONNECT WITH MICHAEL ANDERLE

Michael Anderle Social
  Website:
  http://kurtherianbooks.com/

Email List:
  http://kurtherianbooks.com/email-list/

Facebook Here:
  https://www.facebook.com/OriceranUniverse/
  https://www.facebook.com/TheKurtherianGambitBoo
ks/

Made in the USA
Las Vegas, NV
26 July 2024

92989617R00173